SPELLBOUND MAGIC

SPELLBOUND MAGIC

THE WITCHES OF PRESSLER STREET™ BOOK THREE

MARTHA CARR

MICHAEL ANDERLE

LMBPN Publishing
PMB 196, 2540 South Maryland Pkwy
Las Vegas, NV 89109

First US edition, 2019
Version 1.03 February 2021
eBook ISBN: 978-1-64202-695-5
Print ISBN: 978-1-64202-696-2

THE SPELLBOUND MAGIC TEAM

To the Early Readers Team
Kathleen Fettig
Michael Robbins
Debi Sateren
Michael Baumann

Special shout out to Grace Snokes, Lynne Stiegler, Judah Raine, Kelly O'Donnell and Stephen Campbell for their general badassery behind the scenes to keep everything running so smoothly.

DEDICATIONS

From Martha

To all those who love to read, and like a good puzzle inside
a good story
To Michael Anderle for his generosity
to all his fellow authors
To Louie and Jackie
And in memory of my big sister,
Dr. Diana Deane Carr
who first taught me about magic, Star Trek,
DC Comics and flaming cherries jubilee

From Michael

To Family, Friends and
Those Who Love
To Read.
May We All Enjoy Grace
To Live The Life We Are
Called.

CHAPTER ONE

Emily Hadstrom sat at the kitchen table with one hand wrapped around her coffee mug and the other clutching her phone. She'd played through the news clip twice already and now hit the replay button for a third viewing. "I can't believe this," she muttered.

Her older sister Nickie shuffled into the kitchen from the small dining room, blinking the sleep from her eyes. "Morning."

Emily just nodded but couldn't take her eyes off the screen.

"What arc you watching?" With a yawn, Nickie headed across the kitchen toward the freshly brewed pot of coffee.

"The news…"

"Really?" Nickie poured herself a cup and brought it up to her mouth. "I thought you pinned down local TV news as a waste of time."

Emily blinked at her phone and tilted her head. "Yeah, well, it's just a little different when the news has to do with me."

Her sister nearly choked on her first sip. "You're on the *news?*"

"Not exactly." Emily paused the clip and turned in her chair. "More like something I did."

"Okay…" Nickie raised an eyebrow and moved with a lot more purpose toward the table. She scooted a chair next to Emily's and sat, cupping her mug in both hands and glancing back and forth between her little sister and the paused video. "You really only have two choices, Em. You can either explain why you look like you're about to be sick, or—"

"Yeah, I'll just let you watch it." Blinking quickly, Emily pressed the play icon in the middle of her screen and let the reporter do all the explaining.

"Yesterday afternoon, both the staff—and no doubt a few guests—at the five-star restaurant in downtown Austin experienced quite the surprise at Meadowlark Tavern. I'm here with Ben Calder and his wife Anita, who have a unique take on an even more unique dining experience. Mr. and Mrs. Calder, can you tell us in your own words what you experienced yesterday at Meadowlark Tavern?"

A balding man in his late fifties grinned into the camera while the thin woman beside him gripped his arm, batted her heavily-mascaraed eyelashes, and giggled. *"Sure, sure. Anita and I are… well…"*

"In the lifestyle," his wife added.

The reporter offered the camera a confused smile. *"'In the lifestyle.' Does that mean you're swingers?"*

"If that's what you want to hear, sure." Anita shook her maroon-dyed hair out of her face.

"And did you know you were walking into a...well, for lack of a better term, swinger party *at Meadowlark Tavern yesterday?"*

"Of course not!" Ben's eyes widened. *"That was the best part. There we were, enjoying our late lunch. And halfway through the meal, everyone just started to...really get to know each other, if you know what I mean."*

"Well, not everyone." The man's wife rolled her eyes. *"A few people got really uncomfortable and left. Without even paying for their food. Can you believe that?"*

"But boy, what a time we had. You know, we'd heard of these secret little get-togethers at private clubs or conferences at big hotels. Never managed to make it to one, then bam. *There we were, right in the middle of it, and we had no idea."*

"Just perfect timing, I guess."

The reporter blinked at them. *"Okay, then. And you said you still don't know who this... group is?"*

Ben shook his head. *"Not a clue—"*

"Oh, but if any of them are watching..." Anita gripped his arm tighter and leaned into the camera with an excited grin. *"We would* love *to be invited to the next one. Just find us on Facebook or something. Ben and Anita Calder—"*

"Thank you, Mr. and Mrs.—"

"Whatever we need to do to be a part of it again!" Anita shouted as the camera panned away from her and husband.

The reporter walked away in the opposite direction. *"The Calders are the only participants in yesterday's unlikely event who have been willing to speak with us on this story. It seems the waitstaff and kitchen staff were also completely unaware of the little convention their guests held at the restaurant. As of yet, Travis Macklen, owner of Meadowlark Tavern,* and the head chef of his five-star restaurant, Henry Ansler, have both declined to comment. Back to you, David."

The clip ended, frozen on what looked like the reporter trying not to crack up laughing. Emily stared at her phone.

Nickie tilted her head and frowned. "What… did we just watch?"

Her sister set the phone on the table and slid it away. "Feel free to watch it again. Took me a few times too before it really sank in." Emily blew out a long sigh. "I think it's sinking in."

"What does this have to do with you, though?"

Emily shot her sister a pointed glance and folded her arms.

"Okay, yeah. That's where you work. But it's not like you were a part of this…weird party or anything. I mean, all you do is cook the food…" Nickie knew the minute her sister blushed that she'd hit the answer. Then it sank in for her too. "Oh…Wait, that was *you*?"

"Yeah?" Emily shrugged, wincing. "I just got a little carried away."

"A *little*? Em, you literally cooked up one giant lovefest. For strangers. At your work—"

"I know! I know. It's totally awful."

"And totally hilarious." Nickie folded her arms and smirked. "Honestly, I'm surprised you're not cracking up laughing right now."

"Please don't, Nickie. I'm already embarrassed enough."

"Well *that's* a relief." Nickie shook her head. "Whatever's going on with you, it would be a really good idea to figure out how to control it. Or at the very least tone it down a little."

"Yeah, I know that too." Emily pulled her dark hair back from her forehead with both hands and stared at the frozen news clip on her phone. "I just don't know how, yet."

"Huh. Puts you in a pretty *sticky* situation, doesn't it?"

The youngest Hadstrom sister rolled her eyes. "Don't."

"Come on, Em. That was funny, and you know it."

"I'll laugh about it later when I stop feeling like I wanna go crawl into a dark hole and never come back out."

Nickie snorted. "Hey, it's not like anybody *knows* your magic put a giant dose of free-for-all love potion into the soup..." Her eyes widened. "Did you tell Laura yet?"

"Are you kidding? No, I didn't tell Laura—"

"Tell me what?"

They both turned quickly in their chairs to see the oldest Hadstrom sister standing just inside the kitchen. Laura yawned, and the only sound among them was Emily's gulp. "Morning." Her chair scooted across the floor as she stood and walked around the table. "Coffee?"

Laura smacked her lips and ran a hand through her unbrushed hair. "You read my mind, Em. Thanks." Her youngest sister was already on the other side of the kitchen, banging the cabinet door shut and all but slamming a fresh mug onto the counter beside the coffee pot. "Maybe bring the noise levels down a little, though, huh? And then you can tell me whatever you haven't told me yet."

Emily started humming at the kitchen counter as she poured Laura's coffee, *and* as she pulled the creamer out of the fridge, *and* as she stirred it all in.

Laura glanced at Nickie while taking a seat at the table. "What's she doing?"

"Trying to ignore her life, most likely."

"It's freaking me out."

Nickie shrugged. "Em, I'm gonna show her—"

"Yeah. Sure. Whatever. Here." Emily approached the table, set the coffee in front of Laura, and stepped away like the table might light her on fire if she got too close. "I, uh…I have to feed the dog." She disappeared through the mudroom at the back of the house and into the living room.

Laura frowned. "But our dog's immortal. He doesn't actually need food." She took a slow sip of her coffee, which was just the way she liked it and blinked at Nickie. "So, what's going on?"

"Just…watch this." Nickie pulled Emily's phone toward them and hit the replay icon on the screen. This time, she watched her big sister's expression morph from confusion to shock to dawning, mortified realization. And she tried not to laugh.

When the news clip ended, Laura swallowed and took a deep breath through her nose. "Oh, my god, Emily." She stared at Nickie. "How long did you know about this before I did?"

Nickie shrugged. "A couple minutes."

With a sigh, Laura closed her eyes and took another sip of coffee. Then she stood. "*Em?*"

Her shout made Nickie lean away, and their youngest sister's small, muffled voice returned from the living room. "I didn't mean to!"

"I sure hope not," Laura muttered and headed through

the mudroom. Shaking her head, Nickie stood with her own coffee mug and followed her.

Emily was curled into a ball on the couch, huddled over her knees as she pressed her face into the cushion.

"What are you doing?" Laura asked.

"Trying to disappear."

Nickie chuckled. "Well, that's gonna be a little hard when the entire city's talking about the surprise swinger party that was actually your out-of-control *magic*."

"Nickie." Laura frowned at her. "This isn't funny."

"Hey, taken out of context, it's hilarious."

"But right now, we can't really take anything out of context, can we?" Laura sat on the couch beside her youngest sister and pulled Emily by the shoulders out of her ball of shame. "We have a lot on our plates. All of us separately." She twirled her finger in a circle and caught Nickie's gaze. "And all three of us together. I *would* say the highest thing on our priority list is dismantling nine other energy cores so the Gorafrex can't power them with other witches' blood magic..."

Puffing out a sigh, Nickie lowered herself into the armchair across from the couch.

"But we can't focus on that like we should if something's making our magic go haywire at work and we're feeding customers what might be the strongest love potion I've ever heard of."

Nickie bit back another laugh. "Please tell me you think it's just a *little* funny."

Laura leaned forward to make Emily look at her, and when her little sister gave her an apologetic grimace, she couldn't help but smile. "Okay, yeah. It's a little funny." The oldest Hadstrom sister shrugged. "But it can't keep happening, Em."

"I *know*…"

"So what's going on?"

Emily grabbed a fistful of her own hair and tugged it away from her face. "I don't really know."

"Em…"

"I mean, I was standing in the parking lot, about to start my shift, and John showed up *hours* early just to say hi and basically ask me out on another date…"

"This was *before* Nathan's party last night?" Nickie asked.

"Yeah, it was *before* Nathan's party." Emily shot her a confused glance. "I've been with you guys literally every second since we got there."

Laura leaned forward to catch Emily's attention again. "And?"

"And…" Emily sighed. "I really like him, okay? And Chef Marino basically told me I had to act like I don't even know John at all, because everybody's business is Chef Ansler's business if it's in his kitchen. So I was trying not to act like anything was happening, but apparently I can't keep it together, because then *this* thing happened, and all our customers started… freaking out on each other."

"Or just getting' freaky." Nickie grinned and sat back in the armchair, crossing one leg over the other.

"Seriously?" Emily's shoulders slumped, and she closed her eyes. "So trying not to think about John just made me think about John. And it… I dunno. Went into the food. Again."

"What?" Laura leaned away from her.

8

"What?"

"This isn't the first time?"

"Uh… Laura you know it's not."

"Yeah, but I mean…at the restaurant?"

Emily raised her hands in surrender. "Okay, I get it. You're pissed. I'm reckless and irresponsible. Awesome."

For a few seconds, the living room fell silent. Then Laura burst out laughing. Emily looked at Nickie in confusion, but her sister only shrugged. "Em, I'm not *mad*." Laura's laughter died down, and she grabbed her youngest sister's shoulder to shake her just a little. "I wish you'd told me about this…mass, emotional-magical exposure you're feeding people at work…"

Nickie laughed too.

"Come on, guys." Emily glanced back and forth between them. "I mean, yeah, I see how it's funny, but it really doesn't feel funny right now."

Laura grinned. "That might be a first." Emily stared at her until she gave a small, tense chuckle of her own. "And I think it's an easy fix, right? At least you know what's going on. Kind of. You like John, he likes you, your magic does weird things when—"

A loud thump came from above them, and all three Hadstrom sisters looked up at the ceiling. "What was that?" Nickie asked.

Emily rolled her eyes. "I mean, Speed sleeps in my room. Hey, *Speed*? What are you doin' up there, you—" The jingle of their chubby, immortal, constantly-farting bull-dog's collar came from the mudroom. The dog door clicked back into place as Speed trotted into the living room and toward his witchy owners. "Um…okay."

Laura cringed. "I swear, if that little troublemaker weaseled his way out..."

"What are you talking about?" Nickie asked.

"Huh? Oh, nothing. I just have a—" Another thump sounded, followed by three more in quick succession. Laura stood from the couch, still eyeing the ceiling. "I think that's coming from the roof." The thumping sounded like a hailstorm now, which was incredibly weird for Austin, Texas in the middle of the summer. Then the noise amplified, and it came from all around the house instead of just above them.

"Uh...guys?" Emily stepped toward the large bay windows on the north side of the living room, staring at the small shapes falling from the sky amidst a rain of black feathers. "I'm pretty sure this problem is even bigger than mine."

CHAPTER TWO

"What *are* those?" Laura peered through the bit of window she could see behind her sister.

"Birds." Emily glanced through the window with wide eyes and shook her heads. "Birds that aren't acting like birds at all."

Nickie and Laura rushed to the window for a better look. "Those are grackles," Laura muttered.

"I had no idea that there were this many in Austin." The youngest Hadstrom sister tapped the glass and counted silently. "I don't know. That's gotta be at least a hundred right there in the side yard."

"Okay." Nickie frowned at the dozens of black birds running across the brownish grass and through the bushes outside their house. "Anyone wanna take a guess why we have at least a hundred messengers of the magical world *walking* in our yard? It doesn't even look like their wings actually work."

Emily gaped up at the ceiling. "I think they fell out of the sky…"

"That's ridiculous, Em." Laura shook her head. "The grackles are just as much a part of this city's magical history as we are. And whole…groups like this don't just fall out of the sky."

"Oh, sure." Emily leaned against the window and stared at their grackle-studded lawn. "You guys hear that?"

Nickie and Laura shared a glance, then they both shook their heads.

"Right. Since when have either of you seen a grackle and not heard it screaming nonstop? You think this many of them on the ground and completely silent is normal?"

The oldest Hadstrom sister took a deep breath and tapped her lips with a finger. "Actually, you have a point, Em."

"Thank you."

"Guess there's only one way to find out." Laura headed for the foyer and the front door.

"Remember the last time the grackles found us?" Nickie smirked over her shoulder at Emily. "I mean, it wasn't this many. But still."

"Right, but those could talk." Emily shrugged as they followed their oldest sister out the front door. "And the Tree Folk sent them to us. So that would make them magical messengers and…what? Tour guides?"

"Maybe they still have a message," Laura added as she skirted around the bushes at the front of the house and headed for the side yard.

When all three sisters rounded the side of the house and the sloping hill down to the street, they could hardly keep walking for fear of stepping on a huge black bird no matter where they put their feet. The closest grackles hopped and skittered away from them at first, but not a single black-feathered wing lifted. They stopped at the edge of the gathered birds to figure things out from there.

Laura patted the pockets of her khakis and pulled a fistful of fried crickets from the cargo pocket at her leg. "This might help." She squatted and extended her hand toward the startled, confused birds. A few hopped away, but two decided their sudden inability to fly wasn't worth keeping away from a Hadstrom witch. They approached Laura and cocked their heads, beady eyes taking her in.

"Okay, I know you always like to be prepared," Nickie said, folding her arms with a chuckle. "But when you did start carrying crispy crickets around?"

Laura shook her head and focused on the birds approaching her. "They're left over from some...you know, it doesn't matter right now." Her sisters exchanged a skeptical glance, then the first of the strange-acting grackles got close enough to peck at the bits of fried insect in Laura's hand. "Anything you have to tell us, little guy?"

The bird swallowed the food then stared up at Laura with its beady black eyes. Its head twitched a few times, then it opened its beak to caw...except no sound came out. Over and over, it tried to caw, and nothing happened. One by one, the other grackles milling about on the Hadstrom sisters' yard turned to face the three witches and opened their beaks.

"It's like they're all choking," Emily muttered, frowning at the black-dotted grass full of bobbing, soundless birds.

Nickie shook her head. "This is so weird."

"Yeah." Laura scattered the rest of the crickets on the ground. "It's okay, birds. We get it. Can't fly, and you can't deliver whatever message you dropped out of the sky to give us." She dusted off her hands and stood. "You know, the Engineer *did* say that any of the activated energy cores would do some weird things to magic."

"You think this is from the energy cores?" Nickie's eyes widened. "The Gorafrex only managed to turn one of them on."

"Well, one and a half, technically." Laura rolled her shoulders and sighed. "Looks like that's enough to make these guys lose what makes them *them*. I bet they'd tell us why they can't fly, if they could talk."

"Oh, boy." Emily cocked her head. "Maybe it's something we can help along with a little bit of legacy-ring magic, yeah?" She lifted her hand to cast a spell with the copper legacy ring on her thumb. Both of her sisters clamped their hands on her raised arm and lowered it back down. "What?"

"Not a good idea, Em." Nickie shook her head.

"I said it *might* be from the energy cores the Gorafrex already powered." Laura nodded toward the birds. "But I'm not sure. Not yet. I don't think you wanna be responsible for seriously injuring these guys, right?"

"No, I…I'm just trying to help." Emily frowned at her sisters. "And you guys think I'm just gonna blow them up, don't you?"

Nickie bit her lip. Laura put an arm around her youngest sister and led Emily out of the side yard. "I think we need to know exactly what happened to the grackles before we start experimenting with how to help them. Obviously, we still have a lot of other things to figure out right now too. Like how to get the Gorafrex *out* of whatever human it hops into next."

"Yeah, okay." Emily waved over her shoulder and Laura's arm to the milling, flightless, eerily quiet grackles. "Hang in there, guys."

Nickie came up behind her sisters and nodded. "Locking up the Gorafrex and smashing every single power core left would do them one better, I think."

Laura shot her a quick glance and nodded. "That's the plan."

"Hey." Emily's eyes lit up like two lightbulbs. "You know who's more likely than anyone to have answers about the grackles?"

"No, Em." Laura shook her head and opened the front door before they all stepped inside. "I'm this close to losing my cool with him, and I have a feeling he's just gonna rub the whole thing in our faces."

"But that's what he does." Emily spread her arms, grinning. "And it's hilarious. It's also a good motivator to figure out what we want to know when we go find him to ask."

"You guys are talking about Gilroy, aren't you?" Nickie shut the door behind her as the last one inside and chuckled. "Might be the best option we have right now."

"No. Just...no." Laura raised her arms in surrender and stepped backward.

"Come on, Laura." Emily pointed at the living room windows and the confused grackles on the other side of them. "They need us to figure out what's going on. And sometimes, we need help too. You can't say that snarky bust hasn't given us good information."

"Only after hours of us being heckled first."

Nickie snorted. "Let's just give it a try. It can't be that bad."

"It's *always* that bad. Gilroy is my least favorite family heirloom." Laura folded her arms and pursed her lips. "He does know pretty much everything, though."

"Right?" Emily spun around in the foyer and glanced at the stairway to the second floor in front of them, the small dining room on their right, and the living room on their left. "So where's that jerkface today?"

"Emily, I didn't say I agreed to talk to him right now. Personally, I don't have hours to waste on being called an idiot witch and an ugly pockface and told that my grammar's horrendous." Laura stepped toward the staircase. "I'm gonna look things up the old-fashioned way. In some books."

Before she reached the first step, the staircase slid away from her like a compressing accordion. The walls rumbled around them, then all three sisters were forced to wait in the foyer while their magical house rearranged itself to help them find Gilroy the talking bust.

Laura raised her arms and dropped them in exasperation. "Why do I even try? My sisters, my house...you know, I bet Speed would've done whatever he could to get me to agree to this too."

Emily batted her eyelashes and gave her best cheesy grin. "Just another sign, then, right? That Gilroy's the man we need."

"I don't think he can be considered a 'man' if he's just a head, Em."

"Or whatever."

Laura glanced at Nickie, who just stood in the foyer

and chuckled, running a hand through her long dark hair as the house settled on where they'd find their magical talking encyclopedia. They were still closed off from where the living and dining room usually were, which left them with one option.

"The greenhouse?" Emily raised an eyebrow and blinked. "What's he doing in there?"

"Honestly, Em, I think you're just gonna hurt yourself trying to figure out why Gilroy does anything." Laura passed her sister and headed for the magical addition to their giant Victorian house on Pressler street. She opened the screen door and stepped out onto the tiled floor of the greenhouse, the rest of the place from floor to ceiling made of paneled glass.

"Maybe he wanted some sunshine," Nickie offered as she and Emily came in behind her. "This is the only way he's gonna get it when he can't go outside."

"You know what, maybe we *should* put him outside." Laura gazed at the vines and flowering plants hanging from the frame of the glass ceiling and flourishing in rows of planter tables stretching across the entire room. "Getting pooped on by a few passing grackles would be a good lesson for him."

"Yeah, if the grackles could fly…" Emily tried to hold in her laugh, but when Nickie snorted, it just burst out of her.

Laura shook her head and walked through the rows of plants. "Either of you been in here lately?"

"Nope. Been a little busy with work *and* full-time school." Emily wiped imaginary sweat from her forehead. "Thank the ancestors *that's* over."

Nickie squinted at the watering cans on the table in the

corner opposite the door. "Didn't we set this place up to pretty much take care of itself?"

"Well, yeah. We did." Laura lifted the draping frond of a thick fern spilling over the side of the table and ducked past it. "I just didn't think all the plants in here would've *kept* growing on their own without someone checking in once in a while."

"Looks like we grow some pretty amazing plants, though. Laura, did you put this one in?" Nickie reached out to brush her finger along one plant's purple-and-orange-striped leaves. The first leaf under her finger shuddered and retracted at her touch. The surrounding leaves sprouted fang-looking thorns, and she jerked her hand away before the rest of the plant could rip her finger off. "Jeeze!"

"What?" Laura turned and eyed the orange-and-purple bush, which now looked like a bunch of leaves again.

Nickie blinked at her older sister. "It has *teeth*, Laura."

"No…" Laura squinted, then glanced between her sisters before turning and heading off through the jungle their greenhouse had become. "Probably shouldn't touch any more of these."

"There are *more*?" Emily shied from the luminescent blue vines lifting from a split clay pot and trying to brush against her arm.

"I mean, that's just a guess." Laura shrugged and stepped around a potted bush on the floor with bright-red berries that doubled in size and shrank again, over and over. "But probably."

"Okay. Our greenhouse is now a seriously creepy

jungle." Emily cupped her hands around her mouth. "Gilroy!"

Laura and Nickie ducked and covered their ears. "Too loud, Em. Come on." The oldest Hadstrom sister stopped in front of a tree growing out of the tiled floor. She studied it from top to bottom with a frown, then pushed the branches aside and held them there for her sisters to walk past. "This is…odd."

"You really put those little magic gardeners to work, didn't you?" Nickie stared at the trunk of the tree poking through the tiles, then raised her eyebrows at Laura.

"I wasn't trying to make *this* happen." Laura followed her sisters and gently returned the branches to their rightful place. "But it definitely got a little out of control."

"You think Gilroy just wanted to hide from us?" Nickie asked with a little chuckle.

"You think I give two flying chopsticks what any of you witches think?" On the far side of the greenhouse, under the shade of two massive potted plants with draping vines covered in shimmering silver flowers, Gilroy's marble visage rotated toward them from atop his intricate pedestal. The rumble of stone spinning against stone was surprisingly loud in the greenhouse for how much the overgrowth should have muffled it. The bust sneered at the sisters and blinked in dissatisfaction.

CHAPTER THREE

"*There* you are." Emily laughed and approached the bust. "Enjoying yourself with a little bit of nature, huh?"

"Probably more than you enjoy being absolutely clueless." Gilroy rolled his marble eyes and glanced between each of the sisters. "Who knows? Maybe you're having fun."

Laura shook her head. "This is like when Grandma Eloise made us eat creamed corn that summer we stayed with her. 'It's good for you girls. Eat it, or I'm taking your wands.'"

"Hey, I'd take Gilroy's attitude over creamed corn any day of the week." Nickie gestured toward the bust and shrugged. "At least he stops talking when you walk away. Grandma's cooking wouldn't leave me alone for days."

Emily laughed and leaned toward the bust on the pedestal, propping her hands on her thighs. "We have some questions for ya, Gil."

"If I had a nickel for every time I heard *that* one..."

"You still wouldn't be able to spend 'em, Gilroy." Nickie lifted her hands and wiggled her fingers. "No hands. I'd buy you a nice hat or something, though, if you wanted." Emily turned her head to look at her sister and let out an exaggerated laugh.

Laura sighed. "Okay, let's just get this over with. Gilroy, what happened with the grackles this morning?"

"That is literally the most open-ended question you've ever asked." The bust tilted his head side to side and glanced at the glass ceiling. "I mean, *I* have all the time in the world to tell you everything that happened with the grackles this morning. You'd probably drop dead before I finished."

Laura let loose a frustrated groan. "Why can't you just give up information like a normal database?"

"I like to watch your face turn red."

"You just—"

"Okay, Laura." Nickie patted her older sister on the shoulder. "We haven't even started. This is a process, remember?" Laura closed her eyes and imagined herself in a pristine reading room with all the things they needed to know laid out in front of her in ancient texts that didn't try to hide information. "We just have to try again with another question, right?"

"Right." Emily nodded. "All right, Mr. Gilface. Does the fact that a hundred grackles in our side yard who can't fly or deliver their messages have anything to do with the one and a half energy cores the Gorafrex already powered?"

Laura, Nickie, and Gilroy all blinked at the youngest Hadstrom sister in surprise.

Gilroy snorted. "Yes."

"Ha!" Emily pointed at the bust and turned to her sisters with a proud grin. "That's a new record."

"Well done with the wording, Em." Nickie gave her sister a thumbs up and smiled back. "So now we know that that's the reason. What can we do about it?"

"If you haven't figured *that* out by now," Gilroy replied with a roll of his marble eyes, "you're more useless than you look."

Nickie and Emily cracked up laughing. "You just can't help it, can you, Gil?"

"I can't do a lot of things. Like make you smart, for example."

Laura stepped back. "I don't think I can handle this."

"Laura…" Emily chuckled and grabbed her oldest sister by the shoulder. "He's just a bust. And a magical know-it-all. We've been dealing with that stony attitude since we were kids."

Nickie barked out a laugh. "Good one, Em."

"Yeah, you like that? Just came right out."

"Okay, focus." Laura twirled a finger at them. "If we're gonna do this, let's do it. We can't forget what we still have to do, okay? We have at least eight energy cores to destroy. What I really want is to find the witch-killer before *it* finds a different human host and wakes up their peabrain, but that's pointless if we still haven't figured out how to get the Gorafrex out of its host first. So… let's stay on track." She nodded toward Gilroy and folded her arms.

"We haven't forgotten, Laura." Nickie dipped her head and raised her eyebrows. "We know how serious it is."

"Yeah, it's a little hard to forget when the grackles are as useful as turtles right now for delivering messages." Emily pointed at the marble head that had been giving their family attitude for generations. "There might be a little more room for creative problem solving when we can laugh a few times, right?"

Laura closed her eyes and took a deep breath. "Are the grackles the only things affected by those activated energy cores?"

Gilroy smacked his lips. "Obviously not."

Emily jerked her head up in surprise. "Wait, how is that obvious?"

"We're about to find out." The oldest Hadstrom sister folded her arms. "Gilroy, what else have the energy cores been messing with?"

"Seriously?" The bust raised a stone eyebrow. "Never end a sentence in a preposition, Laura. I've told you this at least seven hundred and twenty-two times."

"That's it." Laura lifted her arms and let them fall to her sides with a smack. "If I keep asking the questions, I'm gonna push him over."

"All right, all right." Chuckling, Nickie lifted a hand to bring her sister back down to Earth. "Em and I can handle the questions. Should I try that one again?"

"Without the preposition at the end?" Laura scowled at the talking bust. "Sure."

"Gilroy, besides the grackles, what else specifically is being affected by the activated energy cores?"

"Everything."

"Okay." Emily nodded, then frowned in confusion. "Straight answer, but that doesn't actually help us very much. Does it?"

"Not really." Nickie ran her hand through her hair again

and tapped her foot on the tiled floor. "Can we reverse whatever magical problem is affecting everything and, specifically, the grackles?"

Gilroy pursed his lips. "It's like a can of Pringles."

"*What?*" Laura shook her head in agitation. "That's not an answer."

The talking bust blew a raspberry at her. "Once you pop…"

"The fun don't stop!" Emily raised a fist in the air, just a little too excited about having understood anther cryptic version of Gilroy's 'help.' "Wait, Gilroy, powered energy cores messing with all things magical in Austin is *not* fun. You know better than that."

"So that would be a no, then." Nickie glanced at her sisters and stuck her thumb out toward the talking head on a pedestal. "I think he's saying there's no way to fix whatever's screwing with the grackles until we destroy all the energy cores. Then we'll just have to figure out the rest of it."

"Yeah, Rutilda *did* say it would get worse the more energy cores the Gorafrex gets its borrowed hands on." Laura tapped her finger against her lips and frowned. "Great. So we go tackle all the energy cores first, and the downside of that leaving the Gorafrex out there, running around in some human's body and making serious trouble by trying to murder a few witches and wizards."

"Or we hunt the Gorafrex first and risk it wreaking havoc on all the magical pillars of the city before we can find it." Nickie wrinkled her nose. "Both options are pretty crappy."

Emily shrugged. "I mean, we *almost* caught it, right?

After that party for Nathan. I still have one of those orbs left, and that pinned the thing down for at least thirty seconds."

"We really need to figure out how to get the Gorafrex *out* of a host before we go up against it again," Laura said. "There's no way to stop it, otherwise, and we don't have the time to fight over and over when we haven't figured out how to win."

"So we go crush some energy cores." Nickie pointed through the glass panels lining the greenhouse, which none of their neighbors had or would ever see. "And we figure out how to get the Gorafrex out of its stolen body. Then we finish this."

Emily nodded vigorously. "Sounds like a plan."

"Or as much of a plan as we can have." Laura cocked her head in acknowledgement. "If those are the only answers we're gonna find, we need to get on it." She turned and headed the way they'd come.

"Thanks for your *tiny* bit of help, Gil." Emily grinned at the bust. "Somehow, we can always count on you."

Chuckling, Nickie waved at the stone head as she followed her sisters through the thick growth of the plants they hadn't tended since moving into the house. "See ya later, Gil."

"Don't let the bushes eat your flesh off on the way out," Gilroy called after them. Then he turned around on his pedestal again, stone rumbling against stone, and stared out at the Hadstrom sisters' empty backyard.

CHAPTER FOUR

L aura stepped along the trail through the Barton Creek Greenbelt in the middle of Austin, heading right back for that willow growing out of the river. "Back to the source, I guess." She hiked through the undergrowth down the steep slope, climbed easily down the boulders she'd been climbing over since she was a kid, and headed across the pebbly beach on the bank of the creek. "There's gotta be something here I didn't see before. I literally have no other ideas for how to put that monster back where it belongs."

It was a lot less exciting to sit and remove her boots before peeling her socks off. "Last time I was here, I couldn't wait to get past those wards." She set her boots and socks in a neat pile on the pebbles, then stood. "This is the first time I've ever regretted going where other people don't."

The green-tinted water was still an excellent salve for the cloying heat in Austin, even before noon. Laura picked her way carefully across the slippery bottom of the creek and headed toward the willow's overhanging branches that had protected the Gorafrex's prison for millennia. The place remained as quiet and empty of people as the day she'd come before as an explorer, archaeologist, and unstoppably-curious witch. "Now here I am again, just trying to pick up the pieces. No. Not just trying. We'll fix this. That's what Hadstrom witches do, isn't it?"

Feeling more confident, she swiped the curtain-like vines aside and stepped into the enclosure made by the willow's branches. Right there, on the little berm built up out of the creek, was the bowl-shaped stone where she'd accidentally released the Gorafrex. "Nothing about this says, 'Dangerous prisoner. Do not tamper.' That might've been helpful."

Laura knelt in front of the ancient white stone and studied it, searching for anything she missed the first time. "And that could be anything. Okay, it's still cracked down the middle, so there's that." She slid her fingers along the edge of the bowl-shaped stone, feeling the time-smoothed surface for anything out of the ordinary. "Just a bunch of dust and vines and dead leaves. What am I missing—oh." Her fingers brushed against a few deep grooves in the back of the stone. "What's this?" She leaned over the stone, but it grew too close to the willow's trunk for her to see much of anything. "Need a better angle."

With both hands around the stone, she pulled it toward her, trying to pry it from the berm so she could study the grooves. Then, she froze. "Yeah, maybe breaking apart a piece of the prison we're gonna use again isn't such a good idea." She sat back on her heels to think, yet it seemed her only option was to get up close and personal.

Her bare feet splashed in the cool water around the berm, as she got on her stomach over the lumpy, uncomfortable ground and brought her face as close as she could to the space between the bowl-shaped stone and the tree trunk. After feeling around again for those same grooves, she kept her fingers on them this time and shoved her thumb into the open space. "I don't have a flashlight or a cell phone, so I need you to help me out here," she told the silver legacy ring on her thumb. "Just a little—"

The ring flashed and almost blinded her with strong light, filling up the entire shaded area beneath the willow's branches. "Close enough." Laura focused on concentrating the light into something she could manage, and the ring responded. She bent her neck at an awkward angle to peer between the stone and the tree trunk for a good view.

"Gotcha. You were put here on purpose, weren't you?" She brushed cobwebs away from the perfectly preserved and deeply cut run in the back of the stone. "Now I just have to figure out what you mean." She reached back for her phone in her back pocket, which she'd left in the car. Phones only distracted her. "But magicals could do all this stuff before cell phones were even a speck of imagination, couldn't they?"

With a deep breath, Laura sifted through her memory for the spell she hadn't used since cell phones came with cameras. "*Capio*," she muttered. Another burst of light flared from her ring, and a copy of the rune—this one made of shimmering golden light—floating up from the space between the rock and the tree to hang in the air for a few seconds. "That's it." She smiled at the full view of the rune. "Now we're getting somewhere." The golden light started to twinkle out, then what was left of it coalesced into a fading streak that shot into her silver legacy ring before disappearing.

Laura stared at her ring, then shrugged. "Probably has better storage than the Cloud. And impossible to hack. Magic is so much better than technology." Grinning, she pushed herself up from the ground, slipping a little on the slick, moss-covered stones of the creek bed before getting to her feet. "I hope this rune can help us." She gazed at the tree trunk and all the willow branches blocking out almost all the daylight. "And then we'll help each other. If I can use this, I'll put that thing back where it came from. I promise."

A breeze rushed over the Greenbelt, rustling the willow's leaves and sending a few branches floating against the backs of her legs. "Okay. Sounds like a deal." Laura blinked and snorted as she turned to leave the berm and the willow and the creek. "I'm talking to trees now. Not that they can't talk back, but still. That's a first. Now I just need to find someone who can tell me what part this rune had to play in keeping a witch-killing creature locked up since this ship was still on its way across the cosmos."

Her first call when she got back in her car was to Carl Hopkins, who knew a lot about magical artifacts and their uses, seeing as he ran a magical antique store.

"Sorry to let you down, Laura." Carl sounded like he was smiling, but his response to her question wasn't quite smile-worthy. "I know a few symbols, but the most powerful runes are beyond me—and anything etched into that ancient prison is *well* beyond my knowledge."

Laura sighed. "I'd still like to show it to you. Maybe you'll recognize it."

"I fear it'd be a waste of your time, but you're always welcome to stop by."

"Okay. Thanks, Carl."

"Good luck."

She stared at her phone, trying to come up with anyone who might be helpful. Her colleagues at the University of Texas had been marginally helpful with information about the Gorafrex. At least, those fellow professors who were also magicals. *One of them was more helpful than the others...*

"No." Laura shouted the word so loud, she startled herself. "No. I am *not* going to ask Nathan for help on this. Especially after the way his welcome-to-Austin party ended last night."

Almost as if she couldn't control her own body, her fingers scrolled through her contacts list anyway and found Nathan's number. She'd even pulled up the contact info before she realized what she was doing. "That's such a bad idea. Isn't it? After my sisters and I ran out on his party to fight a witch-killing monster. After the Gorafrex's next victim was one of his friends. After I actually had fun dancing..." Despite herself, her cheeks grew hot with a blush she couldn't control whenever she thought of Nathan, the half-Kashgar physics professor who happened to occupy the office across the hall from hers.

"Pull it together, Laura. He knows about the Gorafrex now. And the Kasghar helped to build and run this ship. If anyone might know more about runes almost as old as this place, it's him." Butterflies flapped around in the pit of her stomach. "And keeping Austin safe is a lot more important than your stupid schoolgirl jitters." Before she could talk herself out of it, she pressed the call button and turned on the speakerphone. Her hands were too sweaty to risk holding the phone to her face for very long.

"Laura." Nathan's voice had an instant grin in it and made the young witch's heart swell in her chest. "How you doin'?"

"I'm fine. How are you?" *Jeeze. Small talk just isn't your thing, is it?*

He chuckled. "Well, I think I'm doing okay. Just a little confused about everything that happened last night at the party."

"Yeah, about that..."

"Hey, I'm not upset, if that's what you're worried about. I mean, yeah, I'm upset that someone I knew almost got drained dry to fuel that asshole's blood magic, but I don't think I could ever be mad at you."

Laura swallowed, trying to keep her voice even despite how much her racing heart made it feel like she was shaking. *Get a grip. He's cute and arrogant and half-Kashgar. And you're a grown woman.* "Nathan, do you...actually know what *that asshole* is?"

"I do now. Stopped by Vanessa's house this morning, just to check in and see if she needed anything after almost..." He cleared his throat. "Anyway, she told me everything. Definitely wasn't expecting *that* explanation."

"I'm sorry you had to find out like that. I just...well, you understand why I couldn't really say anything about it, right?"

"Absolutely. As far as I can tell, you're handling it way

better than I ever could. But now that the Gorafrex is out of the bag, so to speak…"

She blinked, waiting for him to finish his thought.

Nathan chuckled softly. "Too soon to joke about it like that?"

"What?"

"I said…nothing. I *meant* to say that I'm glad you called. Gives us a chance to talk a little bit more about what happened last night. If you're open to filling me in on the details Vanessa didn't quite have, I'd like to hear it. Plus, I just like talking to you."

"Oh." She winced at the one-word reaction that just fell out of her mouth. *Yeah, you're not really handling this very well.* "Yeah. I guess I owe you an explanation after running out on you like that."

"You don't *owe* me anything, Laura. I just have one question, though."

"Okay."

"Before you and your sisters ran off down the street, did you at least have a good time?"

Laura froze at the memory of how much she enjoyed the party once Nickie and her boyfriend-slash-manager, Chuck, got the music going. "Well…yeah, Nathan. It was fun."

He laughed over the phone. "You know, most of the time, that answer would be a dead giveaway for the complete opposite. But I'm gonna take it for what it's worth. You don't strike me as the kind of person who'd say that if you didn't mean it. At least a little."

Laura puffed out a laugh and realized how much better she felt about this conversation when she laughed—and

MARTHA CARR & MICHAEL ANDERLE

remembered to breathe. "I mean, when we first started talking, I didn't exactly let you down easy."

"That's what I'm saying. You would've just told me the party was awful and you never wanna see me again."

The heat returned to her cheeks. "I didn't say that at all—"

"I know. I know. I'm just messing with you. Sorry."

"Okay." She sighed. "So, can we meet somewhere to... talk? I might also want you to take a look at something for me." *I hope he isn't trying to interpret any of that as inuendo.*

"Yeah, no problem. Is it dangerous?"

"Is what dangerous?"

"Whatever you might want me to look at for you." Nathan took a deep breath, and even through that, Laura heard him grinning. "I don't think us getting together to talk fits that description. Unless that's also part of something I should know..."

"No. No, it's not dangerous." Laura smirked. "Any of it."

"Okay. Great. So, I'm still unpacking all those boxes in my office. Not sure when I'll be done, but if you wanna meet me here, we can go get coffee from there or something. Lunch. Whatever you want."

"Yeah." *Is it coffee or lunch? Or a date?* Laura scrunched up her nose and rolled her eyes at herself. "When can I come by?"

"Anytime. I, uh...have a lot to unpack, actually. Having you drop by is a great reason for me to take a break. Even better when I get to take a break *with* you."

Stop, stop, stop. "All right. I'll probably be there at twelve. Twelve-thirty?"

"Excellent. I can't wait."

"Okay. Bye."

Nathan chuckled, and his voice receded like he was already pulling the phone away from his ear. "Bye, Laura."

She touched the end button and tossed her phone on the passenger seat. "Why did that have to be the most painful thing I've done today?" With wide eyes, she stared through the windshield and caught her breath. "So I'm going to meet with the part-Kashgar professor again. For lunch. Or coffee. I guess it doesn't really matter which one, because he obviously still likes me and—oh, jeeze." She shook her head and started the engine. "You sound like a teenager. Just go do what you have to do." Nodding, Laura backed out of the parking area at the trailhead and made her way to the northern side of Austin and the University of Texas campus.

CHAPTER FIVE

She'd always liked the short walk from the faculty
parking lot to the Liberal Arts building on campus,
where most of the professors and a few instructors in the
Anthropology Department had their offices. Now, though,
when Laura approached the front doors, she couldn't
believe how nervous she was.

*It's just a talk. I can do that. His connections to the Kashgar
can only help, and we need all the help we can get.*

With a reaffirming nod, Laura opened the door and
headed to her office. Nathan's was just across the hall—the
closest open office the Physics Department could offer
once he'd transferred to the university. And right where
she'd be seeing him every day before and after and between
classes once summer was over.

"Stop it," she muttered and frowned herself into
submission.

So when she appeared in the doorway of room A10,
Nathan looked surprised to see her scowling. "Hi!" He

straightened from where he'd been scooping huge stacks of books out of a box on the floor. "Is it twelve already?"

Laura glanced at the Expedition watch on her wrist. *Oh, crap.* "Uh, no. It's eleven-thirty." Her frown morphed into a tight smile. "I wasn't paying attention to the time."

"Oh, yeah?" Nathan chuckled, his eyes with their faint-purple Kashgar glow studying her face. "Or maybe you just couldn't wait to see me again."

"Don't get cocky." She'd meant it as a warning, and the prickly way she'd said it was nothing more than a defense mechanism.

Nathan burst out laughing, shaking his head and stepping around the boxes, totes, and binders littering the floor of his new office. "I've been put in my place." He grinned and stepped close, arms open wide as he bent toward her.

Laura leaned away. "What—"

"It's called a hug." He nodded, smirking at her. "You know, when you see somebody you enjoy being around. Don't tell me you've never been hugged before?"

Pressing her lips together, she stared at him and tried not to laugh at them both. *He's at least a foot taller than me.* "I've been hugged plenty, thanks."

"Oh, so…you don't need any more?"

He was obviously messing with her, but it made her feel like a frigid monster when that wasn't anything remotely close to how she was starting to feel about him. She rolled her eyes and stepped in for the hug.

"*There.* Thank you. I feel better already."

Laura chuckled and shook her head against his chest before they pulled apart. Then she took a deep breath and widened her eyes. "Okay. So, sorry about being early."

"That's a silly thing to be sorry for. Especially when I want you here." Nathan tilted his head and leaned back against the edge of his desk, which was also cluttered with everything imaginable in a physics professor's office.

"Do you wanna keep working on your...stuff." She scanned the mess. "Or do you wanna take that break now?"

He flashed her a wide, careless grin and batted his lashes. "Gee, Laura, I thought you'd never ask." She couldn't help but laugh. "Coffee or lunch? It's a good time for either."

"Wait, you want me to choose?"

"Sure. I mean, we could stay here, too, but I'm pretty sure it's a little too messy, and maybe you're hungry. I am." He shrugged. "Up to you."

"Well, if you're hungry, let's get lunch."

"Excellent." Nathan pushed himself off the edge of the desk and pointed at the door, grinning. "Let's do it."

Laura smiled at his enthusiasm and followed him out into the hall, wondering just what kind of casual, coworker, potentially romantic lunch date this was going to be. *Most of those don't include an explanation of a witch-hunting creature draining the lifeforce magic out of a mutual acquaintance, do they? Yeah, I got this. No big deal.*

They walked a few blocks northwest to the Fricano's Deli on Nueces Street. They hadn't hit their lunch rush yet, so Laura and Nathan stepped inside, got their table in record time, and were greeted as one of three total tables in the whole place. Nathan laughed when she ordered the half sandwich and cup of soup, and she must have shot him a strange look. "Sorry. I just…" He glanced up at their server and chuckled. "I'll have the same."

"Sure. I'll have those right out for you." The young girl, probably a student at the university, smiled sweetly and headed back to the kitchen.

"What's so funny?" Laura stuck her straw in her mouth and sucked down some iced tea just to keep herself from saying anything else.

"I was just surprised. That's all."

"By the fact that we both know how to order good food?"

He grinned and smoothed his hand across his dark, slightly wavy hair. "No, I consider that a good thing, actually. "I just…I don't know. For some reason, I was expecting you to be one of those picky customers who orders but changes everything on the menu. You know, the ones who say not to over-salt anything because they're allergic."

Laura snorted. "I mean, large amounts of salt have been linked to allergic immune reactions."

"Wait, really?"

She frowned at his complete confusion and hoped he was messing with her again. "Yeah…*I'm* not allergic to salt. I think."

"Oh, jeeze." He scratched his arm and stared at the table. "I used to wait tables before I hit the fast track to becoming a professor. Not as fast as you, of course, but I went through pretty quickly. I did have one woman tell me she was allergic to salt, and I thought she must've been out of her mind. Salt being part of the human body, at least."

"Pretty sure it's part of the witch and wizard body, too." Laura smirked. "I have no idea about Kashgar, though."

Squinting, Nathan set his crossed forearms on the table and leaned forward. "Me neither. But I'm mostly human, so you dropping that bit of knowledge on me still applies."

"Well, it's true. Lots of salt and allergies. But I guess it's a good thing I'm not one of those picky customers." She pressed her lips together and stared at the table. *This conversation is already a failure. And we just started.*

They were silent for a few moments. Laura felt Nathan's faint-purple gaze on her face, which was starting to flush with ten times more burning heat than the agony she'd put herself through by calling him. *Say something, Laura. You are a Hadstrom witch and an expert in your field and an adult who doesn't need somebody to prompt her into normal adult conversation. Even if this is a date.* She cleared her throat and tucked her dark hair behind her ear. "It wasn't *that* fast." Slowly, she looked up at him.

He was still smiling, leaning forward over the table like he just couldn't get close enough. "What wasn't?"

"My 'fast track' to tenure."

"You know, I've looked you up, Laura Hadstrom." Nathan grinned. "You got tenure at the University of Texas, your own alma mater, as an archaeology professor when you were twenty-five. Right after receiving your PhD. That sounds pretty fast to me."

"Are you trying to say I rushed it?" Her own boldness surprised her, because now she realized she was actually flirting. On purpose.

"Not at all. That stuff can't really be rushed, so you must have known what you were doing."

"Honestly, it wasn't that hard." Setting her elbow on the table, she propped her chin on her fist and raised her eyebrows. "All it took was finding a few rare, magical artifacts, delivering them straight to the university, and helping the magicals there figure out what the heck those artifacts were for."

"Which, of course, you had no problem doing."

She grinned. "Correct."

Nathan sat back in his seat with a burst of laughter and nodded. "I love how unapologetic you are about it. False modesty doesn't fit you. I'm guessing that's not something you like in other people either, is it?"

She stared at him. Then she narrowed her eyes and asked, "Kashgar can't read people's minds, can they?"

Nathan smirked. "Not that I know. I'm just good at paying attention."

"To me?"

"I hope that's okay."

There was that flush again. *I thought I was getting the hang of this.* Laura took a deep breath and forced herself to smile through her burning cheeks. "So far, I don't think I have a problem with it."

"Then we're off to a good start."

Just when Laura was settling into the realization this was how a date was supposed to go, Nathan brought up the Gorafrex.

"So, like I said, Vanessa told me this morning about what happened. Well, as much as she could for having been abducted and…" He cocked his head and frowned, glancing at the ceiling. "What would you even call that? The thing was draining her? Sucking the magic out of her through a dark-intentioned straw?"

Laura removed her lips from the straw in her iced tea and blinked at it. "That was an oddly eloquent way to put it."

"Sorry. I'm just trying to understand."

"No, that's okay. Uh...I'm not quite sure where to start."

"How 'bout you start with why you and your sisters ended up being the heroes."

She wrinkled her nose. "Don't call us that."

"Why not? That's what you are to Vanessa. The way she tells it, she wouldn't have made it if the three of you hadn't shown up when you did." He rubbed his chin. "Then again, I'm not sure anyone would have a very clear memory of what actually happened, after going through what that woman went through."

"I'm willing to bet she remembers more than enough." Laura shrugged. *She was conscious the whole time. She just couldn't move.*

"Okay, but what about the music?"

Laura froze. "Sorry?"

"Vanessa said Nickie showed up with an electric guitar and a portable amp and...rocked that thing into submission."

A snort escaped her, and she shook her head, looking away from him because she knew she'd burst into hysterical laughter for no reason if she focused on how seriously he was taking this. *And we should take it seriously.* Laura cleared her throat. "I'll tell you what happened as long as you promise not to say, 'rocked that thing into submission' again."

"Yeah, I didn't think that's quite what happened."

"Uh, no that's *exactly* what happened. Vanessa just gave you the simplified version. Can't blame her for that, but there's a little more to what happened than that."

Nathan leaned forward again over the table and sucked a few long gulps of his Cherry Coke. Then he sighed and nodded. "Please, do tell."

"Okay. Just…eat your soup and don't look at me like I'm about to do a magic trick. A *magician's* magic trick. There's a difference."

Chuckling, the part-Kashgar professor spooned up another bite of soup and dipped his head. "I'm all ears."

CHAPTER SIX

"Wow." Nathan raised his eyebrows, blinked, then busied himself with his Cherry Coke while he mulled over the whole story. "That's…"

"I know. It's a lot to take in. But I promise you every single bit of it is true."

"Oh, I don't doubt that at all." He pushed his plate away and leaned back. "It makes sense. I mean, I might be mostly human, but I still have magic. *And* I know all about this ship and how we got…where we are. Not much of a stretch to add a creature who wants to drain witches and wizards of all their magic to power an escape pod and hightail it outta this solar system."

Laura closed her eyes and couldn't keep from smiling. "You have no idea how happy I am that you called it an escape pod."

"That's what it is, right?"

"Yes." *Rutilda would have a few things to say about that, but she's not here, and it doesn't matter.* "So now you know the pickle we're in. And why we ran out of your party without any explanation. It's kinda hard to find the time for those."

"Yeah, especially when your sisters' boyfriends still have no idea what they are and what they can do."

"My sisters'…oh, you mean Chuck and John?"

"Yeah." Nathan ran a hand through his hair and swung his arm over the back of the chair. "I like those guys."

"They're pretty good guys, yeah. And actually, it *has* been pretty hard for Nickie and Emily to keep things on the downlow." She shrugged. "I mean, I don't know how serious things are with Emily and John, but apparently, it's been affecting her work when she…"

"Go on." Nathan folded his hands on the table and didn't quite succeed at looking serious. "Now I'm really interested."

Laura shook her head. "Nothing. That doesn't matter." *He already knows about the Gorafrex, so we can go down that path. But I'm not gonna put all my sisters' secrets out there on the table too. We don't know each other well enough for that.* "Anyway, that's been tricky for her."

"I'm guessing Chuck doesn't know anything, either."

"Nope. Nickie's been with him for years, and he still doesn't know she's a witch. Or that he's got a tiny second brain at the top of his neck just waiting to burst into life."

Nathan nodded, his smile gone—there wasn't anything funny about the Peabrain situation. "That's probably best, though. I mean, if he *does* figure it out, she wouldn't be able to help him much anyway."

"I know. My sister knows that too. She acts like it doesn't bother her, like it's just another *relationship thing* that goes right along with dating her manager. Chuck's practically family at this point, just not…completely." Taking a deep breath, Laura realized how much she'd been talking about her and her sisters' personal lives and wanted to change the subject. *Okay. Apparently, Nathan's just a little too easy to talk to. Keep it casual, Laura. Simple.* "So." She drummed her fingers on the tabletop.

Folding his arms, Nathan sat back. "So."

"Now you know what we're dealing with. And why it's important for us to get on this as soon as possible."

"Yeah, we don't want that thing to take any more hosts or kill any more magicals. Or turn on any more energy cells. You know, I *thought* I felt something funny in the air this morning."

Laura squinted. "What do you mean?"

"Like an earthquake, almost. Except in the air instead of the ground. Sorry. That probably doesn't help with everything else on your plate."

"No, it's fine. That's actually good to know. Something I can recognize, at least, if it happens again. It might mean something."

"Oh. Well, you're welcome, then."

She laughed. "I didn't say thank you." Nathan smiled and blinked those purple, glowing eyes at her. "But thank you."

"Anything I can do to help, Laura."

The butterflies went crazy in her stomach again when he spoke her name, and she glanced away before she turned into a nervous, stuttering, melty witch-mess. "Oh. Yeah, that was the other thing I wanted to talk to you about. What I wanted you to look over for me, if you don't mind."

"Of course not."

"Okay." Glancing around the restaurant, she found the servers all tucked away in the back somewhere and one of the other two occupied tables vacated and already bussed. "Good thing it's a slow lunch."

Nathan shrugged. "Mondays."

Laura focused on her silver legacy ring and willed it to bring up the image of the rune she'd found behind the Gorafrex prison. *Like a magic camera.* Thankfully, she'd focused enough on what she wanted that the ring responded perfectly. The rune projected from her ring onto the tabletop, the golden light glowing there in the ancient shape she couldn't pretend to recognize. "I found this carved into the back of the prison in the Greenbelt. I have no idea what it means, so I'm hoping somebody else does. Have you seen it before?"

Nathan narrowed his eyes and leaned closer to the table, tilted his head back and forth to study the image from every angle. "Not specifically. But the style is familiar."

"Really? That's great."

He chuckled. "I like the way excited looks on you."

Laura blinked, swallowed, and pointed at the glowing rune again. *Focus.* "You think you could point me in the right direction? Wherever I need to go to find out what this rune stands for, I'll go."

"Well…" The part-Kashgar rubbed his lips and nodded slowly. "I think I have a book on ancient pre-orbit technology spells in my office." When he looked up at her, he couldn't keep the small, inviting smile to himself any longer. "If you don't mind accompanying me back to the first floor of the Liberal Arts building."

The glowing golden light disappeared into the silver ring on her thumb. "I should've just showed you the rune the minute I stepped into your office." *Did I say that out loud?* Laura surprised herself and laughed, hoping he wouldn't be offended by any of the things she normally said to herself when she was by herself.

"Oh, hey. Come on. If you'd done that, you would've missed out on excellent company for lunch and riveting conversation."

She tilted her head and playfully rolled her eyes. "I'm glad *you* were riveted. I just want this to be over so all witches and wizards are safe again."

"Plus the Peabrains."

"Plus the Peabrains." *And I'd really like to get my life back. I know Nickie and Emily feel the same.* "All right. Should we ask for the check?"

Nathan aimed a dismissive wave at the table. "I took care of it."

"What?" Laura turned around and looked for their server. The woman was headed right for them again with a checkbook in hand. "No, there it is. Nice try, Nathan, but I'm paying for my own lunch. Thanks anyways."

The server set the checkbook on the table and smiled. "Thank you so much for coming in, folks. Have a great day."

"Thank *you*." Nathan nodded, opened the checkbook, and signed the receipt, leaving a tip as he slid his credit card out and pocketed it.

"Wait a minute." Laura watched their server leave. "How did you… She didn't bring the check."

"I told you I already took care of it." Those purple-tinted eyes glittered as he met her gaze. "And I'd do it again. Hopefully, I'll get to."

Her mouth popped open, and it wouldn't close even when she smiled in confusion. "You haven't left the table since we sat down."

"I slipped it to her on the way in. The Huldu are great at staying hidden, but we Kashgar still know how to skirt by unnoticed too."

"Oh, claiming the whole race as your own now, are you?"

He grinned. "If it makes you look at me like that, Laura, then yes."

"Well… I…" *Literally can't think of anything to say right now.* "Thank you for lunch."

"My pleasure. Care for a stroll?"

They stood from the table and headed toward Fricano's front door. "That's the only way to get back to your office, isn't it?"

Nathan pulled an exaggeratedly mischievous face as he looked at her over his shoulder. "Maybe. Maybe not." He held the door open, and they stepped out of the restaurant's life-saving AC and into the Texas summer steam-cooker.

"Yeah, let's just stick to walking."

"If we were in my old office, I would've been able to pull this out in five seconds." Nathan rifled through the books stacked in boxes and scattered across the floor, the book-shelves built into the wall, and his desk. "See what I mean?" He studied a heavy hardback of something physics-centric and dropped it back into the box. "I've moved a lot and had a lot of jobs. By far, transferring as a professor with my entire library packed in boxes is…" He glanced at the next box beside the first and shook his head. "The definition of insanity."

"You'll find it." Laura didn't want to pry into Nathan's things, but she couldn't help stepping toward the bookshelf and peering at the titles on the not-yet-organized spines. "I'm surprised you keep magical texts in your office."

"Why?" He straightened and looked at her with a goofy smile. "*You* do."

"I…" She turned from the shelf and narrowed her eyes at him. "Touché."

"And I'm not even a-hundred-percent unpacked in my condo yet, either." At his desk, Nathan flipped over books and binders and folders, spreading them out to see their titles. "Just a scattered mess at this point. I'm usually pretty clean when I get settled down into whatever space I happen to occupy at the time."

Laura smirked and turned her attention from the book-shelf to the open box at her feet. "Okay. I'll believe it when I see it."

"Challenge accepted. Hey, feel free to go through anything in here. None of it's gonna bite."

She pulled her hand away from the box just before she would've reached inside to lift out a stack of books. "Why would you say something like that right before I start looking?"

MARTHA CARR & MICHAEL ANDERLE

"Because it's funny. Have you ever been bitten by a book? Be honest."

With a snort, Laura rolled her eyes and squatted beside the box. She gave it one quick, tentative search just in case before pulling out the first few books inside. "No. Nickie did almost lose her fingers to a flesh-eating bush this morning, though."

"Really?"

"A little surprising, I know. We haven't been inside our greenhouse in a *really* long time. I mean, I made sure all the plants were cared for. They're a lot easier to maintain than any of the other creatures in—" She stopped herself before she ended up admitting to the first person in her life that she kept seventeen magical creatures in her walk-in museum closet. "Well, plants are easier than animals."

Nathan eyed her sideways and chuckled. "I'm now keeping a mental list of all the things you stop yourself from telling me."

"Seriously?"

"Just so I can remind you of it when you eventually *do* tell me." He grinned.

"Oh, you're that sure of yourself, are you?" Laura brushed him off and kept searching through the box, pulling out textbooks and peer review journals and something that looked like a DIY advanced-physics-at-home kit. "I'm not sure where I overdid it on the upkeep spells, though. The greenhouse went a little wilder than I expected."

"Maybe that's part of the shift in magic."

She glanced over at him. "You think?"

"Doesn't seem that unreasonable that one and a half

energy cores would make a bunch of grackles drop out of the sky *and* give your greenhouse plants an extra kick. Or bite, as it were."

"Huh. Maybe." The next stack of books she pulled from the box nearly toppled into her lap when the book on the bottom bent beneath all the weight on top of it. *Not a hard-back, then. What's this?* She pulled the other books off the top and found a leather-bound journal in her hands that looked an awful lot like the book of Peabrain magic she'd kept in the drawer of her desk in her own office down the hall.

A wave of her hand over the journal's surface made both her legacy ring and the journal's cover flash a quick, alarming shade of orange. *Oh, great. More wards.* "Is this it?"

"Hmm?" Sitting cross-legged on the floor, Nathan peered up to take a peek. "Hey, yeah! Good find."

"It's warded, so I'm not even gonna try to mess with it. The last time I tried to undo somebody's protection spells..."

He chuckled. "Well, I'm ninety-nine-percent sure there isn't a Gorafrex locked away in those pages."

"Pretty unlikely if they're not iron pages..."

"What was that?"

"What? Nothing. You wanna give it a shot?" Laura held the book toward him, and Nathan crawled across the office floor toward her. One misplaced hand on a book sent the hardcover slipping out from under him. He nearly face-planted right into Laura's lap and caught himself just in time to blink less than an inch away from her thigh. "Whoops. That was...not the way I wanted to join you over here." Shaking his head, he pushed up and stared at the book in her hands. "Sorry."

For the first time since they'd danced at his very professor-like welcome party at Vanessa's, Laura didn't feel self-conscious about bursting into genuine laughter. And it felt good not to worry about what Nathan or anyone thought of her enjoying herself. "You face was priceless, you know that?"

He laughed. "I'm glad you find my humiliation amusing."

"That was more like complete horror." She pointed at her thigh covered by the khaki shorts she'd worn to the Greenbelt and pretty much wore as often as possible. "Like my pockets were gonna attack you."

"I *have* been warned never to underestimate what a witch keeps in her pocket."

Laura patted her side pocket; all of her pockets were empty. "A few weeks ago, I probably would've had my wand tucked away right here, waiting to be used. You might've almost broken it."

Nathan bit his lip in mock embarrassment and leaned toward her. "Please don't tell me you're mad at me for something I almost did but wouldn't have been able to anyway." His purple-hued eyes were closer than they'd been even when they'd danced the night before, though she was only starting to admit to herself it *had* been fun. That purple twinkled, sending tiny fragments of glowing color swirling around his lashes.

They're really beautiful. And most of the world won't ever see eyes like this. "That's a very weird thing to be mad at you about." Laura realized he'd leaned even closer, his gaze moving from her eyes to her lips and back. *Nope.* "So, don't worry about it. And here's your book." She leaned away from him and extended the book with both hands.

Nathan held her gaze a little longer, chuckled, and took the book. "Okay, let's see what's going on with this one."

"Did you forget what kind of wards you put around it?" *Yeah, great way to change the subject. Pretend like he wasn't just about to kiss you...*

"Well, it's an old book." He ran his hands over the leather cover and up and down the spine a few times. "But I'm not the one who put wards on it."

"Oh." Laura watched him study the book. "Have you actually read it?"

"Totally. When I was in high school. My uncle found me with the thing and called me an idiot for playing with old Mechanic technology." With a shrug, Nathan glanced at her and smirked. "Up went the wards, and this beautiful thing went into a trunk of my uncle's secret things."

"How'd you get it back?"

"Uh..." Nathan's eyes widened as he considered how much was too much to tell anybody right now. "Broke into his stuff before I got home."

"You didn't."

"I *did.*" He cocked his head at the journal and leaned forward a little. "I waited seventeen years to do that, and I finally got my chance before the big move to Texas."

"Wow. How old *are* you?"

Nathan snorted and wrinkled his nose. "I'm thirty-four."

All she could do was raise her eyebrows and smile. *Seven years older than me. Seven.*

"Does that completely change the image that I was so desperately hoping to maintain?" He shot her a sideways glance and stopped running his fingers over the book.

Oh, now he's just being coy. "I'm not sure what image you're talking about." Laura shrugged. "But no. Now I just know how old you are. And that's only fair, seeing as you 'looked into me'. You obviously know how old I am."

"Yep. I think it's awesome."

"What's awesome?"

"Just everything about you." He winked and didn't give her any time to respond before tapping every corner of the leather-bound journal in his hand. Silver bubbles released from the tip of his finger and hovered on the surface of the book. When he placed the last bubble of his spell in the very center of the cover, jagged lines of magic cracked across the whole thing, connecting all the bubbles. The journal flashed with orange and silver, and then that was it. The smell of cherries filled the air in Nathan's office, and despite the fact that she'd just eaten, Laura's mouth watered. "Okay. Looks like seventeen years was enough to learn the basics."

"That didn't look very basic to me." Laura couldn't hide her eager smile. *He's good.*

"Coming from you, Professor Hadstrom, that means a lot. Let's find your rune." The journal's spine cracked when he opened to the first page, and they sat on the floor, side by side, seeking a solution to how Laura and her sisters could handle this mess.

CHAPTER SEVEN

Nickie lay on the couch in their living room. One leg hung over the edge of the couch, her bare foot brushing the hardwood floor while the other tapped out a beat on the cushions as she played her Strat. "Something's off." She strummed another chord, followed through the progression, and shook her head. "I can't believe I thought that would work."

Her phone buzzed on the coffee table, and she sat up to answer it. "Hey, babe."

"Hey." Her boyfriend Chuck sounded like his usual, incredibly happy self. "How you doin'?"

"Good. I'm just working on this new song. Trying to, anyway. I haven't had instrumentals give me this much of a hard time in…" She puffed out a sigh. "I don't know how long."

"You'll get it, Nickie. You always do. Maybe take a little break and focus on something else for a while. It'll come to you."

"Yeah, you're probably right." *Except for the fact that*

working on a new song is *the something else I'm focusing on. I need a break from all this energy-core-bashing.* She smiled. "What's up?"

"Just wanted to make sure everything's okay. You booked it out of that party pretty fast last night. And you looked a little…well, I guess those are some bad headaches, huh?"

"They're not fun." *Especially when I hear the Gorafrex's witch-luring drums pounding away in* my *head.* "I'm sorry I kinda ruined the night."

"No, it wasn't ruined. Just…I mean things aren't nearly as fun without you around. We were just getting started."

"I know. It was pretty boring before we got there."

"Go team. But I actually had a decent time after you left. John's hilarious. Nathan's pretty cool in a weird kinda way. Kinda like Laura, actually, so I guess they're a good fit."

Nickie snorted. "Don't tell *her* that."

"Are you kidding? I know what buttons not to push. At least Laura's. I don't know if Emily even has any."

"Oh, they're there. Just buried way deep down under lots of sarcasm and the worst jokes ever."

"Huh." Chuck let out a mocking little whine. "I actually like her jokes."

"You would."

"Hey, are you ready for our meeting tomorrow?"

Nickie took a deep breath and leaned back against the couch cushions. "With Dave? Yeah, I'm totally ready for it. I think it's gonna go well."

"Of course it is. You know, I didn't tell you any of this, just 'cause I didn't wanna overwhelm you. You've had enough on your plate the last couple days."

"You have no idea."

Chuck paused on the other end of the line. "Did something happen?"

"What? Oh, no. Just…you're right. It's been weird, but I think I'm starting to feel better." *Good job, Nickie. Keep up all the lies.* "What didn't *you* tell me?"

"Right. Blue Silk Records isn't the only label who's been pounding on my door trying to sign you. The rest of them, well, they weren't offering anything near what you deserve, so going with Dave is *the best* choice out of the six."

"*Six?*"

"I know, right? Everybody wants Austin's new Queen of Blues."

"Wow." Nickie scratched her head and tossed her hair back over her shoulder. "That's awesome. And I'm ready to do this."

"Great. Hey, I really wanna come over to see you, but I have a few more meetings today. I'm also trying to wrangle all those old dudes into coming on with you when you start recording. They're like a bunch of chickens. Musician chickens."

She barked a laugh. "You still have time for that, though, right? We haven't even signed papers with Dave or anything."

"Yeah, but we will. And I want the band to agree to record with you before they start going senile."

"They're not *that* bad."

Chuck laughed, and the sound of shuffling papers came over the phone. "They're good enough to play with you, and that's what matters. Wanna meet me for lunch tomorrow before the meeting? I feel like I haven't seen you much outside of your shows. Don't get me wrong. I love those. I just...I miss you."

"Me too, babe. Yeah, lunch sounds good. Just text me where you wanna meet." Nickie tapped the dark-blue body of her Strat propped up on the couch beside her.

"Done. I'll call you later tonight. When I'm not herding musical chickens."

"Yeah, okay. Love you."

"Love you, too, Nickie. Be excited! You're signing a record deal tomorrow."

"I've already got the streamers up. The balloons might take me the rest of the day."

"Ha, ha. Good joke. Talk to you later."

"Bye." Nickie tossed her phone onto the coffee table and sighed. "'Be excited.' I wanna be excited. Just a little hard with Gorafrex-possessed humans running around trying to kill our kind and blow this ship to bits with an escape pod..." She leaned on the couch's armrest, picked up her guitar, and started to play.

A succession of taps came from the wall behind her. She kept ploughing through the new chord progressions until Speed noticed the tapping too. The overweight immortal bulldog coughed a little and sounded like he was choking.

Nickie sat up and put her Strat down. "You okay, buddy?"

Speed, ears cocked, paid more attention to that tapping sound coming from the side of the house than she'd ever seen him pay attention to anything. "Oh, are you..." She leaned over her lap to catch his attention. "Is that your *bark*, Speed? I don't think I've ever heard you do that before." The tapping repeated again, faster and more urgent, and Nickie frowned at the side of the house. "What *is* that?"

She went to the window looking out over the sloping side yard and froze. "Seriously? I mean, I get that you can't fly or talk or squawk, but why are you still here?" The tapping continued, but it was quicker and not just a single tap but a *lot* of them. Nickie pressed her forehead against the glass and observed at least a dozen huge, glistening black grackles pecking at the house's siding, all of them in a neat row, trying to chip away at her house. "Hey!" She tapped the glass with her fingernail. "Come on, you…birds. Cut it out."

A single grackle stopped pecking, and the others followed. Now she had a hundred birds in the side yard and twelve of them stared at her with beady, pleading black eyes.

"Leave the house alone, huh?"

If it wasn't so unlike the magical messengers, their response would've been pretty comical. The first one that had stopped the crazed pecking, who was apparently leading the band of misfits, cocked its head, then hunched and turned away from the house.

"Hey, I'm not *mad*. I know this is probably ridiculously frustrating, but I can't think with all that—oh, come on." Each bird in turn hopped away, heads bowed until their beaks almost touched the grass, moving slowly and with obviously hurt feelings. "Jeeze, the grackle walk of shame."

A few of the other birds milling around on the grass hopped toward the back of the house, and Nickie glimpsed Laura's car pulling up along the sidewalk. Her sister practically skipped up the steps to the top of the hill and hustled to the front door in all of fifteen seconds.

The front door burst open. "Nickie! Emily! I found something!" The door slammed shut, and Laura jumped with a little squeak at the unintended force of her excitement. "Hey, guys—"

"Yeah?" Laura jumped again at Nickie's response, and her younger sister just folded her arms and leaned back against the windowsill. "I'm assuming you found something good?"

"Uh, yeah. If we can consider any of this good. But it's helpful. Might even be the part we're missing. Where's Em?"

"I think she went down to the basement. She's been there since you left this morning."

"Doing what?"

Nickie smirked. "Practicing with her metal balls. Or I guess just one of them now."

Laura rolled her eyes and snickered. "We need to help her come up with a better name for those things. Or thing. She still has the gloves I made her, right?"

The middle Hadstrom sister shrugged. "She's figuring something out. Didn't even come up for lunch. I was actually..." Nickie laughed and rubbed the top of one foot with the bottom of the other. "I was actually hoping she'd make *me* lunch. Had to settle for a frozen dinner. Guess I shouldn't start expecting gourmet meals out of her on her days off, huh?"

"No, she really likes cooking for us. Will you go get her? Then meet me in the Clubhouse so I can show you what I found today."

"Why the Clubhouse?" Nickie gave her sister a confused smile. "We're all home."

"Yeah, well, that's where we're keeping our weapons, so...that's part of it. Just meet me there." Laura fingered the silver coin on her keyring engraved with her own thumbprint. The second the pad of her thumb slid onto its twin in the coin, she disappeared from the foyer with a little *pop*.

Nickie shook her head and strode across the living room. "Okay, I get meeting in the Clubhouse to be quiet, or so I can get away from the drums in my head, or so we can pack up our energy-core-destroying supplies, but—"

Laura popped right back into the foyer with wide eyes and shrugged. "Never mind. She's already there. So hurry up."

Laughing when her older sister disappeared again, Nickie went to the side table against the wall the living room shared with the staircase and grabbed her set of keys. "Am I the only one around here who'd like to chill for a little bit? 'Cause we're gonna be *really* busy in like, well, now, I guess. Okay, buddy." She glanced at Speed, and the bulldog slumped to his belly on the floor and nestled his head between his paws with a grunt. "We'll be back soon. Keep an eye on those grackles, huh?" She slipped her thumb over the thumbprint on the round silver keyring, just like each of her sisters', and vanished.

CHAPTER EIGHT

"All right." Nickie stuffed her keys into the back pocket of her jeans and turned around to find her sisters. "So, why's everyone so caught up in...woah."

She found her sisters, all right. Emily knelt on the floor by the huge bookshelf behind the cherry-red futon in the sisters' Clubhouse, her hand raised over the last remaining iron orb Laura's legacy ring had made her as a rather odd weapon. The youngest Hadstrom sister's copper ring glowed on her finger, bringing a faint, translucent red light to the palm she held over the little trapdoor opened within the iron orb.

Laura stood beside her, the iron lance pressed into the ground like a staff wielded by some kind of shepherd queen. She'd raised her hand, too, but this was to cast the spell with the silver ring on her thumb emitting a glowing golden light. This had formed into a shape of curving lens and sharp edges that Nickie didn't recognize.

"Are you guys going after another energy core right now?" Nickie took a step toward them from the center of

MARTHA CARR & MICHAEL ANDERLE

the clubhouse but paused upon seeing the intense concentration on her sisters' faces.

Laura flicked her gaze from the golden rune floating in front of her and cocked her head. "No, but that's not a bad idea, Nickie. You guys have anything going on today?"

"Nope." Emily's eye twitched as she moved the light of her own spell up, down, and sideways over the trapdoor in her iron orb.

"Uh...I don't have any plans 'til tomorrow." Nickie joined them behind the futon. "I'm down to bash one more and score another win for Team Hadstrom, but...what are you guys *doing*?"

Emily jerked her head up, looked at Nickie, and pointed at her round weapon. "Improvements. Obviously."

"Oh, yeah. Obviously."

Laura grinned at her youngest sister on the floor by her feet and nodded at Nickie. "Do you know what this is?" Her finger twitched toward the golden rune in the air.

"Nope." Nickie stared at it. "But you're gonna tell me, aren't you?"

"All right, Em." Laura nudged her sister's hip with the butt of her iron lance. "This is what I wanted to show you, so take a break from your improvements for just a sec." Emily didn't reply, look up, or move to do anything at all. "*Please*, Em."

"Yeah, yeah. I'm coming. I'm done anyway, so..." The youngest sister pushed up off the floor and faced the others. Her eyes widened when she noticed the glowing rune in the air. "Woah. What're you planning to do with *that*?"

"Something I think is actually gonna work for us."

Laura wiggled her eyebrows and smiled up at the glowing image. "I found this rune on the stone in the Greenbelt." She grinned at them like they were supposed to know what that meant.

"There are a *lot* of stones in the Greenbelt." Nickie shrugged. "You might wanna be a little more specific."

"The stone...the *prison*, you guys." Laura lowered her brows at them. "You normally would've picked up on that one."

"I'm a little distracted." Emily glanced at the iron orb on the ball and shook her head before returning her attention to her big sister's presentation. "Definitely keep going, though. This is good stuff."

"Yeah, I think so. I found this rune on the Gorafrex prison in the Greenbelt, like I said. Copied an image of it—"

"So our rings double as magical cameras now, too, huh?" Nickie's lips twitched in an attempt not to smirk at that.

"There is, literally, a spell for everything, Nickie."

"Yeah, and you actually *used* one when it wasn't one-hundred-percent necessary." Emily grinned at Laura, nodding with loads of enthusiasm. "Good work. It feels good to bend the rules a little when you're in a pinch, doesn't it?"

Laura stared at her for a few seconds. "I didn't...okay. Yes. I couldn't go all the way back to my car to grab my phone and all the way back to the Greenbelt to take a picture of the rune. Instead, I used magic, because it was easier." She folded her arms and cocked her head. "Is that what you wanted to hear?"

Emily kept smiling, and she put a hand on her sister's shoulder. "I'm so proud of you."

Nickie snorted.

"Okay, Em. Well, I'm not trying to take all the pages out of your book."

"What's *that* supposed to mean?"

"Nothing. Nothing. Can we focus on me telling you about what I found, please? This is important."

Emily removed her hand and clasped them behind her back. "Yes. Definitely explain this floating, glowing shape."

Nickie just pursed her lips and scratched the side of her head.

"Thank you." Laura peered at the glowing rune. "I'd never seen this thing before, but it had to be on the prison for a reason, right? So, I thought I'd do some digging, and a...colleague of mine"—she swallowed thickly—"had an old journal with a vast amount of information about Arenya V technological magic. A lot of it was about what spells, materials, and magic amplifications the Mechanics used to build this ship, with the Engineers' help; the Kashgar specifically. There was something in there about them wanting to bring the knowledge up to the surface and share it with the passengers, but then things went, well, not according to plan."

"Sucks when that happens," Emily muttered. When her oldest sister shot her a look, she added, "Sorry," and mimed zipping her mouth shut.

"Anyway, after all the explanations of technological magic in this journal, there was a whole list of ancient Mechanic runes used specifically for this ship. I mean, they were probably used for a bunch of other things on Arenya

V, but I think every single one of the runes we found in that journal have been used at some point on this ship. And this one—"

"Who's we?"

"Uh…what?"

Nickie drew her brows together and glanced away from the rune at Laura. "You said 'the runes we found'. Who found them with you?"

"Oh. Just a colleague." Laura's throat tightened.

"Was it Winston?" Emily lifted both her shoulders with a little sigh. "I think he's funny."

"No. It wasn't Winston."

Nickie's mouth popped open, and she pulled in a long breath of realization as a smile bloomed in surprise. "It was Nathan, wasn't it?"

"Definitely not." Laura tried to meet her sister's gaze, but her gaze flickered toward the corner of the Clubhouse.

"Holy cow." Emily folded her arms and echoed Nickie's epiphanic shock. "You did two totally-not-Laura things today that make me just want to pinch your cheeks and give you a big—"

"Stop." Laura raised a hand to ward off her youngest sister's pinching fingers and scrunched up face. Nickie and Emily giggled.

"So you *did* go through a journal of ancient technological runes with Nathan, then, didn't you?" Nickie batted her eyelashes.

Laura tried to stare her sister down, but she couldn't hide the way she felt about the physics professor who might have just handed them the answer to their problem on a silver platter. *Or a leather-bound cover. Either way.* She shrugged. "Okay, fine. Yes. I had lunch with Nathan, then we went back to his office—"

"Hey, *that's* romantic."

"Em…" Nickie shot their youngest sister a warning glance.

"No, seriously. You're both professors, you like being at school, you went to him for help with this rune, and he pulled out a journal that…wait." Emily squinted and studied the ceiling. "Why does Nathan have a journal on Kashgar technology magic?"

Nickie and Laura gave her blank looks, neither saying a word.

"What?" The youngest Hadstrom sister glanced between them. "That doesn't seem weird?"

"Um…" Nickie gestured toward her. "The only weird thing right now is that you're asking that question and genuinely don't know the answer."

Laura's face bloomed a bright shade of pink.

"Okay, I'm seriously missing something." Emily shrugged. "I mean, I know Nathan's magical. Laura told us that when she met him. But that still doesn't explain…oh."

Nickie chuckled. "There it is."

"*Oh…*" Emily turned toward Laura and grinned even wider than before. "I *knew* there was something a little off when I saw his eyes at the party last night. All the"—she wiggled her fingers in front of her eyes—"the purply stuff. That makes so much sense now."

Laura put a hand against her cheek, mostly just because she wanted to feel if her face was actually as hot on the outside as it felt on the inside. "I still don't know if I trust him completely. Not yet. I'm not gonna defend him to you guys if you have a problem with it, but right now, I'm focusing on the fact that he helped me find what this rune means so we can use it on the—"

"Laura." Emily stopped her sister with a gentle rub on the back. "I don't care that Nathan's a Kashgar."

"Part Kasghar. Like way less than half." Laura closed her eyes and shook her head at how much that made her sound desperate to defend him, like she'd just said she wouldn't do.

"Okay." Nickie shrugged. "So?"

"So...the Kashgar aren't known for their overflowing philanthropy, are they?"

"Yeah, but they've been living up here away from their cousins for so long." Emily squeezed her sister's shoulder. "I mean, live around humans enough, you're gonna start acting like them in *some* way."

"And it made them taller, too, didn't it?" Nickie raised her eyebrows.

"Oh, yeah. Nathan's definitely tall. He wouldn't have to be that tall to still have a few inches on you, Laura, but still. You got the whole tall, dark, and handsome thing in one part-Kashgar *colleague*." When Emily's words made her sister chuckle dryly, she joined in. "I don't know why you were so afraid to tell us what he is."

"Maybe I was just afraid to admit that I already knew what he was when I agreed to go to that party with him." Laura scrunched her eyes shut and leaned away from her sisters. "I don't know."

"You know the only thing that upsets me about all this?" Nickie spread her arms, and Laura looked at her with terrified eyes. "That you tried to make us believe Nathan's a dwarf."

Emily threw her head back and screamed with laughter. "Yeah, we saw *right* through that the second he found us in Vanessa's entryway." She wiped tears from her eyes. "That was literally your worst lie in the history of Laura Hadstrom lies. Which isn't that long, actually."

Nickie chuckled.

"So, neither one of you have a problem with me talking to Nathan about our little...our *big* problem?" *I might as well be begging them to let me date the guy. Never had to do that with Mom and Dad, I guess.*

"No way." Emily stuck out her lower lip. "I mean, he pretty much had the gist of it last night when we brought Vanessa back to her house, right? It's not like there was a reasonable explanation for what the Gorafrex did to her. Except for the truth."

"Em's right, Laura. You didn't spill any magical beans, if that's what you're worried about."

"No, but I told him the whole story this morning. I...I mean, I felt like I owed him that much, right?"

"Sure." Nickie approached both her sisters on the other side of the floating rune and set a hand on both their shoulders. "I know this is our *family legacy.*"

"You sound just like Dad when you say it like that." Emily shot her a playful frown.

"Yeah, that's because it was on purpose." Nickie met Laura's gaze and held it. "I know it's *on us* to find the Gorafrex and bring it down. Keep a bunch of Peabrains from waking up after being hosts and going completely nutso on the city with their new magic. Make sure no more witches or wizards die for blood magic." She shrugged and released their shoulders. "But I don't know if there's a way to do any of that without turning to other people for help. Like Rutilda and the Tree Folk. Dad even. Sort of."

Emily nodded. "We'll take all the help we can get. Even from a part-Kashgar who's not that bad of a guy, really."

Laura chewed the inside of her lip and squinted. "What if I end up spending more time with him where I'm *not* looking for his help with our energy-core, witch-killer, Hadstrom-legacy problem?"

"Oh, my god. *Please.*" Emily laughed.

"If you like someone, and you're gonna have a life beyond archaeology and UT and this Gorafrex mess…" Nickie leaned toward her big sister with wide eyes. "Do. It. Laura."

They were all able to laugh at that a little. Then Laura shook her head, but at least she was smiling. "I don't even know what's gonna happen with him. Yes, I'll thank him for helping us, and of course I'll tell him what happens with the rune, but beyond that…I don't know what I'm doing."

"Meh. Nobody does." Emily spread her arms. "Not really."

"Hey, if it helps at all, Chuck said he likes Nathan a lot."

"Nickie, Chuck likes everyone."

Emily pointed at her musician sister. "Actually, that's true. But John even said the same thing. That he thinks Nathan's pretty cool."

Laura raised an eyebrow at her. "I don't know John that well. Does he lie a lot?"

Emily snorted. "As far as I know, I'm the one doing all the lying." She took a sharp breath, blinked at the far wall of the Clubhouse, and frowned. "Aw. That sounds awful."

"It is." Nickie gave her sister's shoulder a gentle nudge. "If you want a human boyfriend who has no idea that magic exists, you're gonna have to get used to it."

After a few seconds of studying her sisters' faces, Laura took a deep breath and turned away. "Okay, that got weirdly pessimistic. Can we get back to the rune?"

"Yep."

"Definitely."

CHAPTER NINE

"We found the rune in the journal. Turns out it's an ancient binding spell. Not like two people bound together, so not, like, a blood pact or soul-binding, also not the kind that replaced super glue whenever this ship was built on Arenya V—"

"You mean it's not *just* technological?" Emily squinted at the floating golden rune in the center of the Clubhouse.

"Exactly. This rune is for a binding spell that holds a living being, any living being, *to technology.*" Laura spread her arms and stepped back, waiting for her sisters to jump around and start celebrating the revelation she and Nathan had stumbled upon a few hours ago. Neither of them said a thing. "Seriously?"

"So…" Emily pointed at the rune. "*That* thing is like the lock on the prison door?"

"Yes. Exactly!"

"And that's what you deactivated when you went snooping around the Greenbelt on your own, huh?" Nickie raised an eyebrow.

"Um...yeah." Laura nodded and gave an apologetic shrug. "I admit I messed up. And I take all responsibility for going in there blind like I did and...unleashing all this on us. I don't think even Carl knew how potent that dagger's magic was in undoing spellwork. Even centuries-old protection wards and that." She pointed at the floating rune.

"Okay." Emily nodded. "That rune is the lock on the door, so when we put the Gorafrex back *into* the prison, we just copy the rune? Reactivate it? Reinstall a new one?"

"Well, yeah. I'm pretty sure that's something we can do."

Nickie opened her mouth, closed it, and took a deep breath. "I don't see how the rune on the prison door is gonna help us get the thing *out* of the human host and *into* the prison."

"Oh. This one won't."

The two youngest Hadstrom sisters eyed each other in shared skepticism.

Laura shook her head. "You guys, if Nathan can help me pick this rune apart into its, well, it's original components, I guess, we can make our own. Put it on one of our weapons and bind the Gorafrex to *that*. With a slightly different rune but one that still has the Gorafrex-as-living-being component."

Both her sisters gaped in realization and let out a long, "*Oh...*" at the same time.

Laura rolled her eyes then let out a sigh of relief. "Finally."

"That's pretty genius, Laura." Emily stared at the floating rune, her eyes reflecting the golden shine as she put the pieces together of what they could do with this information. "Like…that's like solving most of a thousand-piece puzzle and finally seeing what the actual picture's supposed to be."

"Thanks. I think."

"You should keep Nathan around." Nickie nodded and folded her arms. "If he's helping you with stuff like *this*, there's no way you can let him go now. And we should thank him, somehow."

"How 'bout brownies?" Emily's eyes widened as she flashed her sisters an eager grin.

"If he likes 'em. Sure, Em." Laura swiped the loose hair away from her forehead and sighed. "I'm really glad you guys think this is as awesome of an idea as I do. I was starting to think maybe I'd gotten it all wrong."

"You? *Wrong*?" Emily cocked her head. "Come on."

"Okay, Em. So, the next step, I guess, is rebuilding this rune to bind the Gorafrex to iron, which will keep it weak enough for us to get it back into the prison. That's a major problem solved. I'm just not sure yet how we're going to get that thing out of its host first."

"We can't suck it out with a binding spell?"

"No way." Laura shook her head at Emily with a disbelieving frown. "Body-soul binding is *way* more powerful than being-to-technology. Just part of the hierarchy, I guess."

"The bondage hierarchy?" Nickie tried to wipe away her smile, but Emily snorted, then they both burst out laughing.

"Wow. You know, this is why it takes us so long to do

stuff together." Laura shook her head, but a smile flickered at the corners of her mouth. "I could've probably told you everything and laid it all out in five minutes, but nooo."

"Sorry, Professor." Emily pressed her lips together. "I know you're used to silent lecture halls where everyone is riveted to every word you say and nobody interrupts."

"Okay, you have that backward." Laura chuckled and pointed at her youngest sister. "I taught a freshman Anthropology lecture last semester; a room full of eighteen-year-old kids who just moved out of their parents' houses like it was a jail break…that's the polar opposite of paying attention with no interruptions."

"Yeah, that sounds about right." Nickie snickered, imagining her sister's face as Laura gave a lecture in front of two hundred students who'd rather be playing video games and stealing into each other's dorm rooms.

"My point is the two of you are *worse* than that."

All three witches broke out laughing, and Laura felt like she'd managed to pull herself together after a few hours spent with Nathan. *Which almost made me fall apart completely.*

"Okay, okay." Emily grabbed the back of the futon frame and leaned over it, still laughing and trying to catch her breath. "Back to the plan, though. Now that I know we can all make jokes again in the face our *family legacy…*" She frowned and scrunched up her face in mockery.

"Hey, Em. You do a good stern Greg Hadstrom too."

"Thank you."

"The plan," Laura cut in, "is that we keep destroying energy cores. I'll work on designing a new rune to bind the

Gorafrex to a piece of iron. Nickie, I'm assuming you're happy with practicing the lullaby, right? You really rocked that last night, by the way."

Emily nodded. "You didn't look anywhere *close* to passing out that time."

Nickie gave them two thumbs up and a sarcastic grin.

"And what do I work on?" Emily asked.

"I mean, if you wanted to start looking into how to pull a massively powerful force out of a bodily host, that's kinda the last piece we're missing; otherwise, fighting the Gorafrex won't work at all."

"Uh…right. Any ideas where to start looking for that kinda info?"

Laura and Nickie shared a glanced, and the oldest Hadstrom sister shrugged. "You could try the library. There are plenty of other magical beings who use others as physical hosts. You won't find anything about the Gorafrex, though. I already looked."

"Okay. Trip to the library." Emily scrunched up her lips and rolled her eyes away from her sisters. "I'm so excited."

"Laura." Nickie tilted her head.

"Yeah?"

"You still haven't told us the last detail, I think."

"Um…I have no idea what you're talking about." The oldest sister chuckled a little. "And I'm not lying, either."

"You want to put that new and improved rune into one of our weapons, but you never said which one."

"Oh." Laura turned toward the iron lance in her hand, tapped the butt of it against the ground, and peered up at the sharp tip glinting in the light of the magical orbs lining the Clubhouse's ceiling. "I thought this one would be pretty good, right? Nice and pointy."

Emily let out an appraising hum. "I like it."

"Cool." Nickie nodded.

"So." Laura tipped the lance from side to side and eyed her sisters. "Nobody's doing anything today. Wanna go give another energy core—"

"A good smashing?" Emily barked out a laugh. "I'm sorry. I just hear that phrase and think of the Engineer you met under the museum and I just…I mean, it doesn't really make us sound very badass, but whatever. Did she have, like, a British accent or anything?"

"Who?"

"The Engineer, Laura."

"No, Em. She didn't have a British accent. She did speak archaically, sort of. Like a giant Velikan woman who'd built this ship and then spent the last few thousand years under-ground by herself, eating giant cockroaches."

"Gross." Nickie looked disgusted.

"Yeah."

"Huh." Emily blinked and tried not to look disappointed. "I always imagined her with a British accent."

"Nothing's stopping you from keeping up that imagination, Em." Laura patted her on the back. "So, you guys wanna go destroy some ancient technology, or what?"

"Just another Monday." Nickie headed toward the bookshelf on the far wall of the Clubhouse and reached for one of the three matching daggers Laura's legacy ring had made about two weeks ago—it felt like forever. "Let's do it."

"Sweet." Emily stooped to pick up her iron orb and the leather glove Laura had magically crafted as an anchor for the end of the orb's iron string. Then she shot upright and grinned. "Anybody want me to go grab a *teezler* or two?"

"It helped us the first time, Em, but bringing a teezler anywhere is always a bad idea." Laura raised an eyebrow.

"Oh, come on. I feel sorry for the little guys. I can't exactly play ping pong by myself, and neither of you have come to play with me since the first time they destroyed the basement."

"I don't want any teezlers running around when we might run into the Gorafrex. That was a nightmare last time." Nickie twisted the wicked-looking iron dagger in her hand, watching it flash under the light. "But I'm down to come home *after* we break another energy core, and I'll play with you then, if you want." She brought the tip of her dagger down to point it at Emily.

"Deal." Emily raised her iron orb and clinked it against the dagger's blade.

Laura shook her head and replaced the iron lance on the long bookshelf. Then she grabbed the heavy socket wrench the Velikan Engineer had given her as a parting gift; the thing was at least three times the size it should have been, but it packed a serious core-destroying punch. "Only you two would make deals with weapons."

"That's totally not true, Laura," Nickie replied, pointing the dagger at her older sister instead. "I'm sure there were tons of civilizations way back when humans started forgetting about themselves. They probably made deals with their weapons all the time."

"Yeah. Some of them even think they're making actual blood pacts when they cut their palms open and shake hands." Emily grinned and tilted her head. "At least we're not cutting each other, Laura."

"At least there's that."

CHAPTER TEN

"Did you have any particular core in mind?" Nickie asked, swinging the iron dagger at her side as she and her sisters gathered in the center of the Clubhouse.

"Well, that one under Thinkery was pretty important." Laura licked her lips and nodded. "The only other one I mapped out that was around a lot of people with potential for hurting them—or worse—was under the airport."

Emily shook her head. "What are the *odds* of having two of those things under such populated places?"

"One in twelve, apparently." Nickie grinned.

"Well, whatever the odds are, the energy cores were here first." Laura pointed at her sisters. "Our ancestors helped the Engineers build them as part of the escape pod, so whatever just popped up above them when Austin became Austin doesn't matter. We shouldn't let that stop us from doing what we have to do, right?"

"Right."

"Yep."

"Okay." Laura froze and sighed out a self-deprecating laugh. "We can't even go anywhere from here."

"Yeah, maybe we should've thought about that before we built the place," Emily said. "You know, it's great that we can get to the Clubhouse from literally anywhere and carry it with us all the time."

"Don't forget I can get rid of the Gorafrex's drums in my head here, too." Nickie swirled the tip of her dagger and pointed it at Emily.

"Nickie."

"Yeah?"

Laura raised her eyebrows. "Can you stop talking and waving your dagger around? It was made to defeat a witch-killing energetic being. It's sort of distracting."

"Right." The middle sister lowered her weapon and smiled.

"Maybe we should add to the Clubhouse magic," Emily suggested. "You know, make it so we can use the transport bubbles from here instead of having to pop out first and then cast them wherever we appear. 'Cause now I'm gonna have to come all the way up from the basement to get to you guys before we leave."

"Actually, that's a good idea." The oldest Hadstrom sister fingered the silver coin on her keyring and nodded at Emily. "You could work on figuring out how to do that, too, if you want. Not exactly high on the priority list, but it has potential."

"Yeah, okay."

Laura stepped away from her sisters and hefted the giant Velikan socket wrench in her arms. "See you guys by the front door." She slid her thumb over the keyring's thumbprint and disappeared.

Nickie turned to meet Emily's gaze. "Nathan the Kashgar, huh?"

"*Part* Kashgar. That's very important." They chuckled. "Looks like it perked her right up after we told her we didn't give a crap about her making new friends."

"Yeah, she needs a lot more of those." Nickie took a deep breath. "Don't take too long getting upstairs, okay? Laura in go-mode is like a long fuse being lit. We want the Laura bomb to go off where it's supposed to, like on the energy core."

"Aye, aye." Emily gave her sister a goofball salute and slipped her thumb over the Clubhouse keyring in her hand.

Nickie glanced at the ceiling, then she took a few seconds to look around the magical hideaway they had built when they were kids. Nobody in the world could get in or out of this place, including the Gorafrex. "And a teezler, I guess." With a chuckle, Nickie lunged and brandished the iron dagger like a sword. She waved it about for a second, laughing at her imaginary fight with something even she didn't know. Then she stopped, cleared her throat, and nodded at the weapon. "Okay, got that out of my system." Nickie thumbed her keyring and vanished.

When she popped into the living room, Laura was already pacing.

"You okay?" Nickie asked.

"Just ready. Are you ready?"

"Yeah. Emily said she wouldn't take too—" That super annoying tapping came again at the side of the house.

Nickie slumped her shoulders and turned toward the window facing their side yard. "Seriously?"

"What's that sound?" Laura went for the window, making that her new purpose while she had all this problem-solving energy and nowhere yet to focus it.

Nickie rolled her eyes. "The grackles, man. I thought they were bad when they could scream all over the telephone wires, but jeeze. That tapping takes it to a whole new level, doesn't it?"

"How long have they been doing this?" Laura pressed her forehead against the glass like Nickie had earlier and watched the huge black birds pecking at the siding of their house.

"Probably since they fell out of the sky. I got them to stop right before you came home. Apparently, beaking our house is the most exciting thing you can do as a magical messenger who can't fly *or* deliver messages."

"Huh." The oldest Hadstrom sister stared at the birds a little longer, then headed toward the foyer. "When we get back, we should try helping those things."

"Well, I'd love to help 'em. They helped us." Nickie shrugged and ran a hand through her hair. "Any idea how to do that?"

"Nope. We're short on ideas lately, aren't we?"

Chuckling, Nickie wrinkled her nose and bobbed her head from side to side in consideration. "I think the answers we need are the ones that kind of inherently come from doing everything else on our own, you know. Family legacy."

Her older sister rolled her eyes and let out a huge sigh. "Family freakin' legacy."

Just before they could step into the foyer, the magically expanding and contracting parts of their Victorian house on Pressler Street started acting up. A black wall slid into place where the entry to the living room usually was, blocking Nickie and Laura from getting to the front door. Laura tried not to let it irritate her too much. "It's about time."

Walls spun and buckled, sifting one over the other and in every direction along the bones of the house so that Emily had access via the basement. The house stopped changing, Laura and Nickie stared at each other, then heard the basement door—which was on the main level— click shut. Again, the house whirred and groaned and rumbled into a different shape, and the wall blocking the two witches inside the living room lifted into the ceiling and the second floor.

Emily stood there with her glove on and the iron orb in her hand. "Ready?"

"You're gonna use that thing for an energy core too?" Laura asked.

"Totally." The youngest sister grinned. "That bowling ball was awesome when I used it, and this is like a thousand times better."

Laura glanced at Nickie for a little support in voicing their baby sister was making an odd decision. Nickie just shrugged. "We can't say she hasn't practiced enough." Then she went to her sneakers by the front door and stepped into them.

For a minute, Laura didn't respond. Then she blinked. "Yeah, I can't argue with that. Okay. Who wants to kick off the transport bubble?"

"Go for it."

"Yeah?"

Emily and Nickie nodded. The youngest Hadstrom shuffled a little side to side, not quite dancing but standing about as still as Laura was—which wasn't much at all.

Nickie watched her fidgety sisters with growing amusement. *Busy, busy, busy. All the time. I'm so glad I don't get the jitters like that. If either one of them would pick up a guitar—or any instrument at all—I'd love it. Too uptight around here and not enough music.*

Laura lifted her hand and stared at the silver legacy ring on her thumb. "Visualize the energy core. What the other ones looked like. *And* that it's under the Austin Airport, okay? We wanna make it to the right one."

Emily offered her sisters another ridiculous-looking salute.

"No problem," Nickie said.

With the barest hint of a thought, Laura's ring picked up on what she wanted to do. The luminescent, swirling bubble formed on the top of her ring and grew to the size of an orange before disconnecting from her hand. It floated between the Hadstrom sisters and, in under a minute, became big enough to fit all three of them inside.

The witches stepped into the bubble, shared a determined glance, and visualized their destination.

CHAPTER ELEVEN

The bubble popped, and they looked around in curiosity.

"Okay." Emily summoned a glowing white orb from her copper legacy ring and floated it toward the ceiling. The light drifted and illuminated the high ceiling of the passageway they'd entered, however far underground they were. "I know we were just in one of these last night, but I'm creeped out a little by these chambers."

"Really?" Laura and Nickie shared a confused glance.

"I didn't know you got freaked out by anything, Em."

"Well, I mean not freaked out like *scared* or anything." Emily hefted the iron orb in her hand and headed away from her sisters down the curving corridor. "Just like...that thing's been down here for a *really* long time, right? It's creepy that all of this looks abandoned and forgotten and that none of it works anymore."

"I'm pretty sure that's because all of those descriptions are true," Laura said, following her youngest sister as Nickie came up behind them.

"Yeah, I know that. The whole world just forgot about this totally awful thing our ancestors put away in this prison, in the very center of Austin, and sure, maybe things are almost on the way to not working at all. Except the energy cores. We already know those can be activated. But can you imagine what it must've been like for that thing? Locked up down here, inside iron walls for centuries. I don't even know what it's like on the inside, but the outside isn't that awesome. The Gorafrex knew that the whole ship was moving on through time without it, but that wouldn't have mattered. It was just…down here."

Laura swallowed and wished she didn't so easily empathize with what her sister was saying.

"You can't feel sorry for it, Em." Nickie tightened her grip on the iron dagger.

"No, I don't feel sorry for it." Emily's lower lip turned down in denial. She shook her head. "I'm just trying to *imagine* what it would be like. I mean, I know none of *us* are gonna live anywhere close to a couple thousand years, but still. That would make it even more pissed and even more dangerous, don't you think? It snuck onto the ship and got caught. Whoops. It got stuck in jail, which yeah, would seriously suck too. But then to just be *forgotten* about…like it took the three of us longer than it should have to even figure out what the Gorafrex really was."

"I hear ya, Em." Nickie nodded and caught sight of the opening into the energy core chamber on their left.

"We shouldn't have been *able* to forget it in the first place," Emily continued. "Something that powerful that wakes up human Peabrains after using their magic *and* that wants nothing more than to kill witches and wizards specifically for the kind of magic they give up when they die. How does anyone forget about *that?*"

"You hit on one of the major questions of history everywhere, I think." Laura followed her youngest sister into the massive chamber, where the energy core rested in the metal cradle built in the floor. The glass-like structure of the core's clear column rose high above them, connecting into another metal cradle attached to the ceiling. Nothing else in the chamber but the core. No flashing lights, no Gorafrex, no witch about to be sacrificed for the creature's eventual escape. "You think the Gorafrex has been to every single one of these by now?"

"I'm not gonna pretend to know what that thing wants or how it checks off whatever boxes exist for 'suitable to activate first with a witch's lifeforce magic.'" Nickie stopped a few feet away from the energy core and gazed up its smooth surface. "But it knows who we are now, doesn't it?"

Laura swung the massive Velikan wrench at her side. "Yep."

"And it knows what we can do," Emily added.

"It's gonna be coming for us. Eventually." Nickie shook her dark hair away from her face and took a deep breath. "We still have a lotta work to do."

"We'll get there." Laura turned to face the middle Hadstrom sister and nodded toward the energy core. "Wanna take a stab?"

Emily guffawed on the other side of her. It echoed through the chamber, and she covered her mouth.

"Ha, ha." Nickie lifted her iron dagger. "Take a stab.

Actually, I'm good with just staying here and letting you two have all the fun."

"You sure?"

"Yep. Destroy away."

Laura and Emily exchanged a look, but neither of them argued. "Em?"

"*Yeah.*" The youngest Hadstrom sister grinned and turned her attention to the iron orb in her hand. Her finger pressed down on the little button on the top of the sphere, and the trapdoor clicked up on the bottom. The super thin, weirdly flexible iron chain spilled out of the opening, and Emily grabbed the end with her half-gloved hand so she could rest the chain against the metal panel Laura had added to the palm. "Really great invention, by the way."

"Well, I kinda owed you one."

"Yeah, you did. I like the glove. No more bloody hands for me." Emily only had to think about sealing the end of the chain to the metal panel in her glove before her copper ring flashed. The two pieces of metal bonded into one seamless part. "Honestly, it's super weird that my orb broke the way it did last night. That it didn't snap off here"—she pointed to the metal plate on her glove— "but just pulled right out of the actual ball part."

"That's probably cuz we still need to find out how to get the Gorafrex out of its host," Laura replied. "You wrapped it up perfectly with that…what are you calling it now?"

Emily smirked. "The Strangler."

"Uh…cool. That thing did its part last night. We just weren't fast enough 'cause we didn't know how to get the Gorafrex out of the human."

"It was always meant to be a temporary hold, huh?"

Emily lifted an eyebrow at her iron orb and shrugged. "That's cool, I guess. I'm not about to do anything temporary to this energy core though." Lifted out of her contemplative mood, the youngest witch turned toward her sisters with a massive grin and an exaggerated wink. She took a few skipping steps away from the energy core, wound her arm back, and launched the iron orb toward the center of the glass-like column. She'd been practicing so much it felt like second nature to cast the spell with her copper ring to propel the orb with more force than remotely possible without magic. Even before the flash from her ring subsided, the orb smashed through the clear column—in one side and out the other. Shattered fragments of whatever material this was—none of the sisters thought it was true glass—tinkled down into the center of the core.

Emily hadn't prepared for gravity taking its course. Her iron orb reached the end of its tether, and the chain caught on the edge of the second hole it had made. The round hunk of metal swung downward with a loud, echoing bang against the glass, and Emily was jerked across the chamber floor by her hand—with the glove and the iron chain attached to it.

She shouted, her Converse sneakers squeaking across the floor, and right before the iron orb pulled her farther than she could go, she released the chain from her glove with an explosive flash of light from her ring. The string slithered up the side of the glass column, the iron orb fell to the chamber floor with a resounding *thud* and echo like a struck gong, and Emily slammed into the base of the energy core.

For a few seconds, the entire room fell silent, then

Nickie and Laura rushed toward their sister. "Oh, jeeze. Em, are you okay?" Laura reached out for her, but the youngest Hadstrom witch pushed herself off the black cylinder and blinked. When she stepped back, a light-blue glow shimmered along the outside of the core where she'd smacked against it. The same magical light pulsed along Emily's forearms, chest, and stomach, and then faded.

"I'm...fine." She looked at her sisters with a spreading smile. "Definitely didn't expect *that*. But I guess my trusty sidekick took care of everything else for me."

Nickie snickered, then cut it short when she remembered how not funny any of this was. "Your sidekick?"

"Your *ring* did that on its own?" Laura grabbed Emily's hand and took a close look at the legacy ring on her thumb.

"Well, hey. I probably deserve a little credit, don't ya think?" Emily grabbed Laura's hand, catching her sister off guard, and shook it curtly. "Maybe I'm quicker on my feet than I thought."

"Everyone with the awful jokes today." Nickie let herself laugh. "You were definitely moving across the floor."

"And my reaction time was perfect. Put up a cushioning shield right before I hit this thing." Emily slapped the side of the energy core, eliciting a high-pitched echo that vibrated the length of the clear cylinder. "*And* I managed to disconnect from my weapon that *turned against me*." She glared at the iron orb, which had rolled a little from behind the huge energy core and lay in a coil of iron string. "That went better than I thought, actually."

"I think maybe you've been practicing a little too much,

Em." Nickie chuckled and patted her sister on the shoulder. "You really rocketed that thing."

"I mean, I gotta make sure I do it right. Next time we end up fighting the Gorafrex, the last thing I wanna do is miss."

"Okay." Laura took a deep breath. "Just as long as you don't blow a hole through the human host in the process, okay? Maybe tone it down."

Emily glanced up at the two jagged holes in the energy core's cylinder and shrugged. "Yeah, okay." Then she went to collect her orb from the chamber floor.

Laura hefted the massive wrench in her hand and stepped backward, eying the energy core. "Anybody mind if I just…"

"Go for it!" Emily shouted, lifting her weapon again and cradling it under one arm.

"All yours." Nickie stepped back and watched her older sister lift the wrench to take a good swing. "Hey, maybe keep a tighter grip on it than last time, huh?"

"Well now that I know what it can *do*…" Laura stuck her tongue out, then lifted the wrench a little in front of her. "Kinda like putt-putt, right?"

"When was the last time you played putt-putt?" Emily folded her arms.

"Probably the last time you went bowling, Em."

Emily let out a long string of fake laughs until both her sisters eyed her long enough to make her stop.

"Just pretend it's a club." Laura swung the wrench with a little more force than she'd ever swing anything on a real putt-putt course. The Velikan wrench hit the metal cradle of the energy core with a metallic *ping*, and a blue light flashed on contact. A massive crack splintered up the side of the core from metal base to metal ceiling attachment. When the crack reached the height of the two holes in the clear cylinder, the entire tube of glass-like material shattered, raining toward the witches. "Okay. Let's go." Laura tightened her grip on the giant socket wrench and booked it.

Emily gazed up at all the twinkling shards falling in slow motion. "Looks like teeth just fallin' out of someone's mouth…"

"Emily!" Nickie shouted.

"Yeah." She turned and ran after her sisters before the wave of jagged, fractured glass smashed into the ground.

The sisters made it all the way out of the chamber and into the curving hallway before a rumble louder than any sound a fallen energy core had made filled the corridor. It came from above them. All three ducked in response before slowing and turning to gaze at the ceiling.

"What's going on up there?" Nickie asked.

"That's…" Laura cocked her head, listening to the high-pitched whine of the engines and the squeal of tires over tarmac. "Holy crap. That's a plane."

"I don't think I've ever flown in a plane and heard it make that sound." Emily glared at the ceiling. "So why is that one—"

The floor of the corridor rocked beneath them, shuddering and tilting upward slightly. Laura caught a stumbling Emily, who was only concerned about keeping her iron orb in her arms so it didn't roll away down the buckling hall. "What the heck?"

The air filled with muffled, shouting voices coming

toward them—not from the underground hallway but from the surface. "Okay, we've never destroyed an energy core and had all this craziness happen at the same time." Nickie spread her arms. "Did we do this?"

"I don't think so." Laura's eyes widened. "I'd say either the Gorafrex activated another one, or whatever's going funky with Austin magic is getting worse."

Nickie shook her head and stared at her sister. "I didn't hear the drums."

"I don't know if that means anything. Assuming you always hear them when the Gorafrex is about to kill another witch or wizard…"

"It's the magic that's already been knocked out of normal." Emily grimaced. "I thought it only got worse when another energy core turned on."

"I don't think Rutilda knew what she was saying most of the time during our little chat. She was kinda losing it." Laura twirled her finger by her ear, glancing at the ceiling beneath so much noise and shouting. "I have a bad feeling about what's going on up there. We should go."

"Yep." Nickie nodded at the translucent transport bubble growing to full size in front of them.

The sisters met each other's gazes as they stepped through the thin magical membrane. "Home?" Laura asked. The others nodded, then they all disappeared.

CHAPTER TWELVE

The bubble burst in the Hadstrom sisters' dining room, and Laura stormed across the foyer into the living room. "Whose phone is this?"

"Mine." Nickie followed her, and Emily set her iron orb on the dining room table before joining her sisters.

Laura snatched Nickie's cell phone off the coffee table and handed it to its owner. "Pull up the news."

"Uh...yeah. Crap. Okay." Nickie's fingers were a little slippery as she tried to settle them on the right numbers for her passcode and pull up the internet browser. *Slippery fingers. Jeeze. Great for playing gigs. Totally the wrong thing for trying to work a smartphone.* Finally, she had the browser up and froze. "What news?"

"I don't know." Laura whirled and paced the living room. "Anything that's covering the airport right now."

"Oh, my god." Emily clapped her hands to her cheeks and dragged them down her face. "Please just let it be a normal mechanical malfunction."

"Not sure those two things go together, Em." Nickie

typed in the first thing that came to mind—'malfunction at Austin airport.' A list of basically the same headline turned up on her browser. "Okay, so there's Fox 7, ABC 13...Jeeze, you look it up." She shoved her phone at Laura, who tossed the huge socket wrench aside with a loud *clang* against the hardwood floors. Emily winced and Nickie stared at the giant tool turned weapon.

Laura did a better job of keeping her cool and found what she'd hoped she wouldn't. "Oh, man." Her eyes moved back and forth across the article. "No..."

"Any time would be a good time to tell us," Emily muttered.

"It's bad."

"Laura."

The oldest Hadstrom sister looked up and couldn't keep the remorse off her face no matter how hard she tried. "They *are* calling it a mechanical malfunction..."

"There's a but in there somewhere," Emily said, searching her sister's gaze. "What's the but?"

"But it's not just contained to one plane."

"Crap." Nickie ran a hand through her hair and blinked. "How many?"

"Twelve. So far." Laura swallowed and set her sister's phone on the coffee table. "Different airlines. Same issue. And, by same issue, I mean nobody's been able to figure out what happened to the planes."

"But what happened?" Emily chewed on her fingernail.

"They just kinda...dropped out of the sky." Turning around, Laura slumped onto the living room couch and brought her hands to her temples. "Arrivals and departures. Some of the planes lifted off and just dropped.

Whoever was coming in and trying to land? Dropped. I didn't see anything about casualties, but still."

Emily sank into a squat beside the coffee table and hooked her fingers over the edge. "It's not just the grackles."

"Sounds like anything in the sky." Nickie sat on the edge of the armchair across from the couch and bent, resting her forearms on her thighs. "If it's the same thing that dropped the grackles this morning, that means it wasn't us. We didn't make anything worse by breaking the energy core under the airport, right?"

"I don't think so." Laura rubbed her forehead and puffed out a sigh. "I hope this is just Austin. If this stuff is happening anywhere else, there are zero other magicals who have any clue as to what's going on. They're totally in the dark."

"It *could* just be Austin." Emily nodded encouragingly. "That's where the escape is. Just Austin. That's where our family's been since this ship set off from Arenya V. Nowhere else. Why would magic start giving people serious trouble anywhere else if everything's *right here*?"

"No idea, Em." Laura blinked at her hands. "It's too soon to tell one way or the other, but I don't think we have the time to figure it out. We need to keep going with this."

"Yeah. I'm with you." Nickie stood from the armchair and nodded. "We didn't run into any human-possessing witch-killers just now. And there are still seven other energy cores pretty much untouched."

"As far as we know," Laura added.

"So, let's go get as many as we can. That one wasn't hard. We get in, get out. If the Gorafrex shows up, we have transport bubbles and the Clubhouse as a last resort." Laura snorted at that one, and Nickie stepped toward her. "I'm serious. It probably won't show up. It's only been a day since we saw it last. Maybe it's still looking for another human, but until I *do* start hearing alien beats in my head again, we should finish what we started."

Emily swung her head one more time from Nickie toward Laura and waited for an answer. When it didn't come, she offered, "I'm down to keep going. Got nothing else to do for the rest of the day."

"Okay. Yeah." Laura nodded and looked at them. "We'll take care of as many as we can right now. I'll start working on the rune tomorrow." She stood and, this time, Emily lifted her hand to let her copper legacy ring do the work of casting a transport bubble.

While it grew to its intended size, Laura raised her hand and projected through her ring the map of Austin she'd put together, complete with the purple lines of the city and the yellow dots of all twelve energy cores she'd located. "So, anybody have a preference for the next one?"

"Totally up to you." Nickie pulled at her earlobe and studied the glowing magical map floating in their living room.

Emily blinked and jumped toward the far wall beside the couch. With a grunt, she lifted the Velikan wrench her sister had been hauling around and slung it up against her shoulder. "Seriously, this is the most important part, isn't it?"

"You want your ball and chain?" Laura smirked at her own pun when Nickie let out a subdued giggle.

"Naw. At least, as long as you don't mind sharing with

your sisters and taking turns playing bash the ancient-technology piñata." Emily shrugged.

"No problem." Laura pointed at one yellow dot on her map—the next one moving clockwise from the airport. "This one, okay? Right in the Walnut Greenbelt."

"Yep."

"Got it."

"Okay." Laura removed the map with a wave of her hand, then turned and stepped into the transport bubble. Her sisters followed, and she took a deep breath. "Remember, just—"

"Visualize the energy core," Emily said.

"*And* the Walnut Greenbelt," Nickie added. "At the same time. I think we've got the hang of this Peabrain magic by now, Laura. At least the transport bubbles. I don't know about everything else."

"Well, I do still have a whole book on Peabrain magic." Laura smiled at the Velikan socket wrench propped on Emily's shoulder. "I bet we could learn a few things from that when this is all over."

"We gotta get it done first." Nickie nodded and pressed her lips together. "Let's go."

CHAPTER THIRTEEN

J ust after 8:00 p.m., a luminous transport bubble burst into existence in the Hadstrom sisters' living room. It burst, and Laura, Nickie, and Emily stood there, haggard and exhausted and a little discouraged. Emily, in particular, was soaking wet. She stalked across the foyer, through the small dining room, and into the kitchen without a word.

"Come on, Em." Laura followed after her. The Velikan wrench came down on the dining room table with a *thunk*. "I had no idea it was a water line."

"Uh...Laura?"

"What?" She turned around and spread her arms at Nickie, who followed her sisters slowly and cautiously through the house. "I'm trying to apologize."

"Maybe just leave it alone for like, I dunno, half an hour or something?" Nickie widened her eyes and glanced into the kitchen.

"Yeah, but..." Laura frowned and lowered her voice to a whisper, jerking her thumb over her shoulder toward the kitchen table. "Yeah, but then she gets to be mad at me for half an hour."

"Better than a couple days like last time." Nickie's mouth drew down into a nervous-looking line as she eyed Emily.

The youngest Hadstrom sister was opening and closing cabinet doors and kitchen drawers like it was the only way to play Whack-A-Mole. She muttered to herself, clearly angry and clearly trying to calm herself down by cooking something.

"Right." Laura blinked and walked toward the foyer. She stopped beside Nickie and whispered, "Don't eat whatever she's making right now."

"Yeah, I know. I have no desire to be angry for no reason other than just wanting a gourmet snack. I haven't forgotten how Em's magic works." Nickie shot her sister a confused frown. "Are *you* okay?"

"What? Totally. I'm fine." Laura passed her and went into the living room. She settled into the armchair, crossed one leg over the other, and closed her eyes.

Nickie leaned back toward the kitchen and the sound of Emily cursing under her breath while whatever she was handling jumped and thumped and rocked all over the counters. "You need any help in there, Em?"

"That's up to you," her sister shouted, not even bothering to hide her frustration. "But I can't promise that the next person who walks into this kitchen won't get their fingers accidentally chopped off. You know, 'cause the Hadstrom sisters apparently have *the worst aim ever*!"

Grimacing, Nickie turned slowly around, kicked her shoes off by the door, and headed into the living room. She picked her dark-blue Strat off the couch cushions and slumped in its place to strum a few chords. Laura didn't look at her, which was more aggravating than Emily throwing a little fit in the kitchen—which wasn't exactly unfounded.

Nickie stopped playing and stared at her sister. "Laura."

Laura sighed and shook her head, staring at the area rug beneath the coffee table. "Okay, look. This whole thing is overwhelming. But we knocked down *three* energy cores today. Just us. And that giant Engineer bashing club." Nickie nodded toward the dining room and the Velikan wrench resting on the table, hoping that would crack a smile on her sister's face. It didn't. "Nobody expects you to be a hundred percent certain and a hundred percent right all the time. You know that, don't you?"

Laura closed her eyes, took a deep breath, and leaned forward so she could arch her neck and back to stretch some kinks out. "I do."

"What?"

"*I* expect myself to be certain and right. All the time."

"That's not even...*nobody* can do that."

The oldest Hadstrom sister rubbed the back of her neck and shrugged. "Most of the time, I'm pretty certain. Which is great. I used to be right when I was sure of something. That's what got us into this mess. I was sure there was something behind those wards in the Greenbelt, and yeah, I was right about that, but then I screwed up and let that thing out. First Hadstrom in thousands of years to get anywhere near it since the witches who put it in that prison. And I let it out."

"Okay. Please don't turn this into a pity party." Nickie

set her guitar aside and pulled her legs up to cross them beneath her. "That's not what we do, Laura. You know that. And the way I look at it, there are more cores in pieces right now than standing. That's pretty good."

"We still have the one that's already been activated. And the one that got at least a little bit of Vanessa's lifeforce magic before we destroyed it. And now there are planes falling out of the sky."

Nickie tried hard not to smile, but it wasn't possible when she remembered how they'd bashed in the other two energy cores the last five hours. "I don't think Emily's mad about the planes falling out of the sky."

Her sister scowled. "I had no idea crushing that last one would make that pipe explode. The energy core was in a new neighborhood, for crying out loud."

"Yeah, built on top of an old neighborhood." A chuckle escaped Nickie, and she bit it off. "You didn't do anything wrong. Just remember that. I mean, do you even know *how* to make spraying water curve around the corner and hit anything in a different room?"

Laura blinked, then her lips twitched into a half smile. "I bet I could figure it out."

That made them chuckle. Nickie ducked when the oven door slammed in the kitchen and Emily let out a curse. "Don't tell her that. She knows magic's acting super weird right now. She knows you didn't have anything to do with spraying her down like a dirty animal."

"Hey. Mom used to wash us off with the backyard hose when we were kids."

"Well, maybe Emily's working that out for herself now."

Nickie bit her lip. "She did always cry like she'd just fallen off her bike whenever Mom pulled out the hose."

"Weird. We used to get dirty on purpose, just so she'd break out the hose and march us around the yard." Laura relaxed under the memory of those summers when they were all young enough to have someone else clean up their messes for them. "Wish this whole thing was as easy as breaking out the hose."

"I think it's called adulting." Nickie cocked her head and gave her sister a smile that was more joking than sympathetic.

"Good one."

"You know, if it keeps being this easy to destroy the rest of the cores, we can have the rest of them done this week." Nickie's smile faded when she remembered what the rest of her week looked like. "Or maybe...I dunno. We'll hafta work around this meeting I have with Chuck and Dave tomorrow and the shows I'm playing Thursday and Friday."

"I hope music still works the way it's supposed to by then."

"Hey, don't even joke about that." With wide eyes, Nickie jabbed a finger at her older sister. "Seriously. First, I'd be crushed and would come home and do some angry tension-release like Em. Second, if that happened, Laura, how the heck are we supposed to fight off the Gorafrex?"

Laura blinked, sheepish for a few seconds, then burst out laughing. "I can't believe I didn't think about that. Me! *I* didn't think about what would happen."

Nickie didn't know whether her sister was losing her mind or finally undoing the mask she maintained by always being firm and determined, *certain and right*. But they laughed together. "I feel like maybe we shouldn't talk about the hypothetical worst-case scenarios of magic going sideways. That's gonna give me nightmares."

"I thought you never remembered your dreams?" Laura narrowed her eyes, still smiling.

"I don't. Doesn't mean I don't have them. But seriously, I don't want to—"

"Okay, you two," Emily called from the kitchen. "Before either of you say anything, I'm opening this with an official peace offering, okay?" She stepped into the living room carrying a massive plate of Funfetti cupcakes with chocolate frosting. Her sisters stared at her.

"Who do we know who's turning ten?" Laura asked, sharing an amused glance with Nickie.

"Couldn't tell ya. I mean, Funfetti's...*fun*." They all snorted at that. "But I don't think it actually has a flavor, does it?"

"Ha, ha. You're both so hilarious." Emily stopped beside the coffee table and set the plate down within reach of everyone. "Like I said. Peace offering." She looked at Laura and shrugged. "I know you didn't do it on purpose."

"Well, thanks, Em. That's good to hear." Laura glanced at the cupcakes. "I still don't think it's a good idea to eat anything you made while you were angry. Even if it wasn't at me."

"No, no. You can eat them."

Nickie leaned forward. "Didn't we just watch a video this morning about what happens when people eat what you cook under the influence of intense emotional distractions?"

"Hey, that's different."

Laura folded her arms and sat back in the armchair. "How's that?"

Emily flung her hand toward the cupcakes. "Those aren't from scratch. Are you kidding me?"

"How do we know that's true?" Nickie raised an eyebrow and tilted her head.

"Oh, yeah. I put all my incredible magical cooking skills to good use baking you guys Funfetti cupcakes. World-class talent at its finest. Thanks a lot."

Laura and Nickie burst out laughing, and Emily shook her head. "Okay. So…eat the cupcakes or don't. Whatever. They probably taste like packaged mix and chocolate that doesn't have a shelf life. The point is, we're good." She eyed Laura sideways. "Right?"

"Yeah, Em. We're good."

Nickie sucked in a sharp breath and clenched her eyes shut. "Uh, no."

"What?"

"We're not so good."

Emily frowned. "Hey, I thought you and I were always cool with—"

"Em, stop." Laura stood from the armchair and knelt in front of Nickie, who gripped both sides of her head. "It's the drums, isn't it?"

Nickie grimaced and let out a slow, shaky sigh through clenched teeth. Then, she nodded.

"Crap." Emily scratched her head and ruffled her hair. "Clubhouse, then, right?"

"Yeah. Nickie, where are your keys?"

Nickie leaned to the side and reached for her back

pocket. The Gorafrex's ancient, primal drumbeat exploded in her head, and she swayed, coming close to falling forward off the couch.

Laura caught her by the shoulders and kept her steady. "You got it?"

Nickie tugged her keys from her back pocket, and she got the round silver charm separated from her keys. The drums got louder and more urgent, pounding faster and faster with the rhythm that went way back in the Hadstrom family line. She grunted, and her keys slipped from her fingers.

"Okay. *I* got it." Laura retrieved her sister's keyring, singled out the Clubhouse charm, and grabbed Nickie's hand. "Just...like..." The second she slipped Nickie's thumb over the thumbprint, the middle Hadstrom sister vanished. Laura slumped against the front of the couch, grasping for a second at nothing but air when the keys and her sister's hand were gone. "That was weird." She glanced at Emily and shrugged. "Never had someone pop right out of my arms." Then, because that sounded so ridiculous, and because they had so many things on their plates right now, Laura burst into laughter and buried her face in the couch cushion.

"So..." Emily glanced around the room. "I'm gonna go with her. You okay?"

Laura nodded and waved her off, unable to talk through her hysterical laughing. *Am I starting to lose it?*

"Okay. You should come too." When she got no other response, Emily thumbed her keyring and disappeared.

Shaking with unstoppable giggles, Laura reached into her own pocket for her keychain and had to stop to wipe away the tears pouring down her cheeks. "You got this, Laura." The sound of her own cracking voice made her laugh all over again. After a few seconds, she pulled herself together, stared at her keyring, and blinked through watery eyes. "At least I'm laughing. Don't know if that's better or worse than freezing up around Nathan. But, whatever. We have a whole bunch of other stuff to get done first. Like finding which human the Gorafrex just jumped into this time." That thought sobered her. She slipped her thumb over her coin and popped out of the living room.

The dog door in the mudroom flapped open, and Speed squeezed his chubby body through the opening. His nails clicked on the hardwood floor as he trotted across the living room. Despite having lived for almost as long as this ship had been caught off course, his sense of smell was still as strong as it had been when he was a pup. The bulldog cocked his head at the sound of a few grackles pecking at the side of the house, but the smell of something he knew wasn't meant for him made him ignore the birds. They wouldn't be able to tell him anything anyway, not as they were right now.

With a simultaneous snort from both his nose and his rear end, Speed followed the scent to the coffee table and found its source on the plate of cupcakes covered in chocolate frosting. He might have been a magical, undying pet, but he certainly wasn't more immune than normal dogs to the opportunity of a treat left alone.

CHAPTER FOURTEEN

Nickie blinked at the ceiling from where she lay on the cherry-red futon in the Clubhouse. "I was *just* talking about how I haven't heard the drums since last night and how that *thing* is still out there trying to find somebody to...stupid..."

"Hey, it's not like you jinxed someone or anything like that." Emily sat cross-legged on the floor in front of her sister. "The Gorafrex is gonna do what it's gonna do if we talk about it or not. Which we should, by the way, seeing as we're trying to stop it and everything."

"Yeah, Em. I know." Nickie rubbed her forehead and pushed slowly up to sit against the futon's upright cushion.

"Are you sure you're ready to—"

"Sit up on my own?" Nickie raised her eyebrows at Laura and couldn't help but smile. "I'm pretty sure I can handle that much. If I can pull my car into a gas station with this happening, I think sitting's covered."

"Okay, just...take it easy." Laura sat in one of the ratty, horridly-colored armchairs they'd squirreled away as kids, yet sitting still was almost as bad as sitting on a rosebush. "You think that's what it was, though? That the drums were from the Gorafrex finding a new host and not...you know."

"What?" Emily turned to glance over her shoulder. "Are you talking about killing another witch. Or wizard." Laura shot her a quick frown. "You are, though, right? I just wanna make sure I have this straight."

"Yeah, Em. That's what I meant."

"It's gonna be hard for us to get very much of anything straight, honestly." Nickie ran a hand through her hair and sighed. "But I'm pretty sure it was the whole 'new human host' drums and not the whole 'lure a witch or wizard into my clutches' drums. Not the 'power an energy core with my victim's lifeforce and blood magic' drums, either. I mean, they all sound the same, but there's a pattern, right?" She swallowed under her sisters' attentive gazes.

One of the dozens of magical origami animals they'd made as kids—a paper jellyfish the size of a baseball—lifted from its resting place beside an old lava lamp—that somehow still worked—and fluttered across the room. It headed for Nickie, and she leaned away.

Emily raised a finger, her copper ring flashed, and a spark of yellow light leapt from her fingertip to bat the irritating childhood creation aside. "Keep going." She set her elbow on her crossed legs and cradled her chin in her hands.

"Thanks, Em. I mean, I know we've only come across these things happening a few times. Hopefully, we can keep it to just a few, but it's been the same thing since we found the Gorafrex in the first host."

Laura wrinkled her nose. "That super tall guy with the ponytail and the fringed vest."

"Yeah, he was *not* happy about his peabrain waking up." Emily's eyes grew wide. "I'm pretty sure he thought he was tripping acid or something."

"I'm pretty sure he already knew what tripping acid's like." Laura cocked her head at her youngest sister, paused, and frowned. "You don't, do you?"

"What? No. Don't be like Mom. But no." Emily rolled her eyes and turned to Nickie. "Talk about the pattern."

"Yep. Drums when the thing leaps out of its used-up host. That was the first time I heard them *in* my head. Drums when the Gorafrex is trying to find another victim. Drums when it's looking for a witch or wizard who doesn't know they're being lured into a trap. Which is pretty much all of them." Nickie shook her head and jumped back onto her train of thought. "Drums pretty much any time the thing uses magic and, especially, when it's trying to power up an energy core by killing one of us."

"Nothing you can't handle with your Strat and a portable amp, huh?" Emily wiggled her eyebrows, just trying to lighten the mood, and Nickie couldn't help but crack a smile.

"Thanks, Em. Last part of the cycle. The drums get really sporadic when the human host is running out of power, I guess. Right before the Gorafrex needs to hop out and find another one. Just in little bursts when there's not enough of whatever it is to keep the thing inside the person's body *and* using its magic. Then it balloons out, like we saw, and there's a newborn Peabrain in an adult body with no idea what's happening, and the witch-killer flies around Austin a few more days to find another host." Nickie frowned and chewed the inside of her cheek. "Except this time, it only took a day. Like not even twenty-four hours."

"Do you think that means anything?" Emily asked. "I mean, besides the fact that it's getting to know the ins and outs of the city."

"Come on, Em." Nickie gave her sister an almost imperceptible shake of the head.

"Hold on." Laura stopped pacing the other side of the Clubhouse and came to stand beside Emily sitting on the floor. "Whether or not that was meant to be a joke, Em, I think you have a good point."

"I do?"

"Yeah. So that first house. The witch's house where we found the bloody symbol on the wall and the second host right before she woke up…"

"Yep. I don't think any of us forgot about the house."

"Okay, so I was going off the assumption how that witch's house was on top of an energy core. That's how I mapped the rest of them out, with the Greenbelt in the middle. Turns out I was right 'cause the transport bubbles took us exactly where we wanted to go, which was any one of those dots on my map."

"And?"

"And that thing took a couple days inside the second host to find a witch it could use as its first…victim. Man, I hate saying that." Laura folded her arms and shifted her weight to one side. "I think it was probably looking for an energy core first and just got lucky an unsuspecting witch lived right above where it wanted to take her in the first place. So far, it's had three hosts, and it *just* left the third one last night. It's been out for two weeks."

"It's staying inside them longer," Emily offered.

"Right. And it's taking less time to find a new one. I mean, that first time we cornered it in the parking lot was probably a fluke. The thing panicked, and another human happened to be walking out of that store at the worst possible moment."

Nickie frowned, putting the pieces together, then looked at Laura with wide eyes. "You think it's learning about Austin from its *hosts?*"

Laura shrugged. "I mean, why not? It's using their Peabrain magic. Riding off of the abilities none of them knew they had before it slipped into their skin. If it's connecting with them enough to access their dormant magic, it's not that far of a stretch to think the Gorafrex can read their minds too. Or something like it."

"So now it knows where to find other witches and wizards, just like that." Nickie's hand fluttered in aggravation. "It snatches them up, and then it knows how to blend in and act like nothing's happening when it takes the next one into another house or another public park or wherever the other energy cores are."

"I bet you it's canvassing the neighborhood too." Emily nodded, her eyes narrowing as she stared off into space just to the left of Nickie's head. "Or neighborhoods, plural, I guess. Looking for the next host *and* the next magical. Is it smart enough to plan things out like that?"

"Didn't seem like it at first," Laura said with a shrug. "I'm pretty sure that was the rush of suddenly being free after thousands of years. Maybe a little panic too. But, yeah, Em, I'm sure the Gorafrex is smart enough to make plans. It already knew about the escape pod on this ship, and it already knew what it had to do to activate the cores."

"Anything that hunts down witches and wizards to feed on their magic as its sole purpose *has* to be smart enough." Nickie grimaced and leaned back against the couch. "We need to figure out how to interrupt the plans of a thing that's had thousands of years to make them."

"We're already doing that, right?" Emily straightened and glanced at her sisters in turn. "Destroying the energy cores. That's messing with its plans."

"That's keeping it from powering the escape pod and getting off this ship. Plus, taking everyone with it in the process." Laura shifted her weight to her other foot. "Rutilda said only half the energy cores needed to be powered for the Gorafrex to leave. We destroyed six, but one of them's been activated already."

"So, we smash up another one first," Nickie offered. "Later, though. After the last of this headache goes away, and I can get in my own bed without any more drums."

"Sure. Tomorrow, then?"

"I have that meeting with Chuck and Dave."

Laura nodded. "Okay. Tomorrow night?"

"I'm going out with John," Emily said with a shrug. "Made those plans a few days ago, and I'm not gonna back out of a date with this guy."

"Okay." Laura tossed her hair out of her face and nodded. "You guys go do what you need to do tomorrow. I'll work on making the new binding rune. How about Wednesday?"

"After my shift's up, sure."

"Nickie?"

"Yeah, I'm free on Wednesday. No problem." Nickie reclined on the hard futon cushion and draped her forearm across her eyes. "I'm gonna hang out here a little longer, make sure things die down all the way. The drums'll be gone eventually."

"I'll stay with you." Laura stepped toward the futon. "I'm not gonna be able to focus on anything tonight anyway. I'm exhausted."

"Then go to bed. I'm fine, Laura. Really. Thanks."

"Okay." Laura made a pouting face her sister didn't see and bent over to kiss Nickie's forehead. "If you need anything—"

"I'll Sister Soup you, okay? Don't worry."

"Okay…"

"Well, *I'm* definitely going to bed." Emily pushed to her feet and smacked a wet, noisy kiss on Nickie's forehead. Her older sister frowned, chuckled, and wiped her head without moving her forearm from over her eyes. "Good night." Emily thumbed her keyring and left the Clubhouse with a magical pop.

When she reappeared in the living room, another wave of exhaustion washed over her. "Maybe I shouldn't have turned to angry baking as soon as we got home." Emily went to get the cupcakes she'd left on the coffee table…but they were gone, plate and all. "Um…" She spun in a tight circle and frowned. "Great. I really wanted one." Laura appeared behind her, and Emily turned and pouted at her sister. "You didn't eat those cupcakes, did you?"

Laura eyed her skeptically. "I thought they were a peace offering."

"They were but…I mean, they weren't all for you."

Laura pursed her lips. "You think I'd eat *all* those by myself?"

Her sister shrugged and glanced around. "You were here for five minutes after Nickie and I both went to the Clubhouse. You *were* the sixth-grade hot-dog-eating champion, I remember that much."

"Emily, I couldn't eat a dozen cupcakes in five minutes if that was the only way to lock the Gorafrex up in its prison again."

The youngest Hadstrom sister lifted an eyebrow and dipped her head. "Really?"

"Okay, if it was that easy, yeah. I'd totally cram them down. But I didn't even eat *one*. I promise."

"Did you move them, then?"

Laura smirked and folded her arms. "Em."

"Yeah."

"How do you lose a plate of cupcakes?"

"That's what *I* wanna know." Emily bent and glanced at the floor under the armchairs. "It's really starting to…" Her gaze moved under the coffee table, and she dropped to her knees with wide eyes. "You've gotta be kidding me." There was the plate, sitting on the area rug with zero cupcakes on it. She grabbed it, slid it out from under the table, and showed it to Laura. "This. Did you see him before you came to the Clubhouse?"

"I've barely seen him at all today. He doesn't really have much of a defense, though, huh?" Laura pointed to the smears of chocolate frosting and the single piece of incriminating evidence—a chocolatey pawprint smudged at the edge of the plate.

Emily pushed to her feet and shook her head. "That can't be good." The empty plate dropped onto the coffee table, and she stalked off toward the mudroom and the back door. "*Speed!*"

Laura grabbed the plate and headed toward the kitchen to put it in the sink. "I hope it was worth it, you crazy dog."

CHAPTER FIFTEEN

The Gorafrex had not hunted freely in a long time. The creature relished such freedom now, though none of its recent human hosts fought as hard as this one did. *'Be still!'* The Gorafrex raged into the mind of the man it had taken. There were no words given as response—only a high, panicked scream muffled from somewhere far away in the human's subconscious. And the man struggled mercilessly.

"A familiar place..." the Gorafrex murmured through human lips. It blinked borrowed eyes and took in the building on Colorado Street, outside of which it had taken its host the previous night. The human fought so hard the Gorafrex had not been able to walk farther than a few feet from those front doors. *'I chose you because you are strong,'* it shouted in the man's mind. *'Do not prove me wrong.'*

The host's eyes flashed silver, and the Gorafrex walked in another's skin through the entrance to the building. It had picked the pieces from its hosts' memories—who they were, where they'd been headed, what they'd wanted

MARTHA CARR & MICHAEL ANDERLE

before the Gorafrex awakened their forgotten second brain. "And when I'm finished, you'll remember none of it," he whispered. "So stop fighting me."

A strong, suntanned hand reached out to press the call button in the lobby elevator. The Gorafrex waited for the transportation box, which took patience on the creature's part; yet, not nearly as much patience as it had stored away for centuries trapped in the prison of iron and magic. The Gorafrex grew stronger by the day, fueled by the humans' innate abilities and by the use of their magic that allowed it to soon escape from this place. It wasn't as strong as it had hoped to be, after thousands of years without practice or sustenance, but almost.

When the elevator doors opened, the human stepped calmly inside, as the Gorafrex rifled through memories and knowledge, all laid out like photographs scattered across a table. He pushed the button for the seventh floor and waited to be delivered to what the host called *his office*.

"And when you feel safe enough to submit to me, surrounded by your life and the things you know and cherish, you *will* stay put until I'm finished with you." It was a harsh whisper, though the Gorafrex and its host were alone in the elevator.

Finally, the bell dinged, and the elevator doors opened into the busy lobby of some human company. Phones rang, computer keyboards clicked beneath swift fingers, and the man stepped from the elevator to head for his office.

"Good morning, Mr. Mackler." A human in a shiny silver dress-suit nodded and smiled.

The Gorafrex grunted and moved past her, sifting through its host's memories and simultaneously searching for the door the man knew as his own. When they reached the office, he stepped inside, shut the door silently behind him, and took in everything about the room—new to the Gorafrex, familiar to the man.

An image of some blue, shimmering material waving in the wind had been painted on the wall adjacent to the windows. The entire back wall was glass, looking out over downtown Austin on a warm, sunny summer day. Cars and people and magicals passed below them on the street, unaware of the Gorafrex's presence above.

"Not for much longer…"

With all the confidence of a creature on its way to escaping the confines of a ship that should never have held it, the Gorafrex walked toward a large mahogany desk with its back to the windows and an expensive executive chair behind it. He ran his hand along the back of the leather chair. "This calms you, does it not?" He rolled the chair away from the desk, and the man sat where he'd been sitting every day for the last five years. With a sigh from both Gorafrex and human, who wouldn't remember any of this when the time came for them to part, he leaned back and set both arms on the armrests. "Just a while longer, then. Until you accept this is where I will remain."

CHAPTER SIXTEEN

"Nickie, will you stop pacing like that?" Laura sat at the kitchen table, arms folded, and frowned at her sister walking back and forth beside the counters.

"Yeah," Emily added with a snort. "You're acting too much like Laura right now."

"What's that supposed to mean?"

"Oh. Nothing." The youngest Hadstrom sister busied herself prepping the chicken Caesar salad she was making from scratch for lunch.

"You just focus on your cooking, Em." Laura shook her head. "I'm not interested in eating a lunch that'll end up making me comment on everyone else's business but mine."

"You don't need my magic overload for that one," Emily muttered.

"What was that? I didn't hear you."

"Nothing, Laura. I'm zipping up now." Emily pulled the lettuce apart and pressed her lips together.

Laura eyed her for a minute, then laughed to herself

and peered at Nickie. "You're making *me* nervous, Nickie."

"*You're* nervous?" Nickie didn't look at either of her sisters but stopped pacing and poured a glass of water from the tap. She downed the whole thing and slammed the glass the counter. "You're not about to have one of the most important meetings of your career right now at the same time that some alien witch-killer is running around in a new host. Who knows when it's gonna start up with the drums again?"

"Wait, are you nervous about the meeting or about the Gorafrex?" Emily turned partly around, brandishing her chef's knife. "Because neither of those things sound like something that would make you nervous."

"They're not. Normally. But if I start hearing the drums and freak out and have to run out of there so I can pop into the Clubhouse without anyone seeing me..." Nickie widened her eyes at Laura, spreading her arms. "That's not gonna make me look like a musician who's ready to take things to the next level, is it? So forgive me if I'm pacing. I learned it from the pacing guru."

Laura studied her sister, trying to figure out exactly where all this nervous energy was coming from. The last time she'd seen Nickie nervous was on their first visit to Park N Pizza as a family, and she wasn't scared of the rides or the crowds. She'd been terrified and excited and out of her mind when they found out Willie Nelson was playing a set that day. "Who's this meeting with?"

"Dave." Nickie started pacing again. "I told you that the other day, didn't I?"

"Chuck's friend Dave?"

"Yeah, Chuck's friend. But I'm not having a meeting

with his friend, Laura. I'm having a meeting with Dave Mackler, owner of Blue Silk Records. That's who he is today. Not Chuck's friend, not my friend, not anyone who's gonna go easy on me because I just happened to *have a bad day*. Which he can't even imagine, because he'll never know what's happening, but it wouldn't be cold feet or me having a nervous breakdown; it would be the...*stupid* drums in my head, and I would completely lose my—"

"Nickie?"

"What?"

Laura leaned and pulled a chair out and patted the seat. "I think you should sit down for a sec."

"I don't..." Nickie frowned at her sister, then turned to eye Emily. The youngest of the three witches kept busy with her cooking yet shrugged. "Fine." Nickie slumped into the wooden chair, leaned back, and pressed both hands against her forehead. "This is literally the worst timing."

"Hear, hear!" Emily thrust her knife into the air before bringing it down on more chicken breast.

"It's bad timing for all of us, Nickie. And you'll be fine." Laura held her sister's gaze and nodded. "Have you heard the drums since last night?"

"No."

"Okay. Good. That means there's a little time before the Gorafrex starts making any more trouble."

"Maybe." Nickie sighed and ran a hand through her dark hair. "I told you what this meeting's for, right?"

"Nope. But I can guess."

"Blue Silk wants to sign me. Dave wants to sign me. Get me in the studio and record a single and a full album after that, and I'm pretty sure that's where I've wanted to be."

"You deserve it," Emily added, nodding over the counter.

"Thanks, Em."

"She's right." Laura grinned. "You know, I wasn't sure about the record-deal thing. That that's what you're doing today. Don't most people kinda jump around all excited and have some kind of celebration?"

"I think that happens *after* the papers are signed…which may or may not happen today if I have to dash out claiming massive migraine *again*."

"Everything's gonna work out." Laura glanced at Emily. "And after all the papers are signed, we'll celebrate."

Emily turned around with wide eyes. "*You* wanna party?"

"Why is that so surprising?"

Nickie chuckled. "'Cause you don't. Just like I don't jump around all excited and squeal and do weird happy dances."

Emily snorted and returned to her cutting board. "Lots of weird things happening lately."

"Okay, well, maybe we all need to get out and decompress, right? We got three energy cores yesterday, and that was rough. And we're not even close to done. Honestly, I wouldn't mind unwinding a little."

"Really?" Now that the conversation had turned away from her impending record-deal meeting and the hypothetical interruption of it, Nickie felt better about dissecting whatever was going on in her big sister's head. "Does that have anything to do with Professor Nathan?"

"Oh, please." Laura rolled her eyes and sat back. "Why does everything have to come back to him?"

"Because that's something we should celebrate too, right?" Emily did a little dance at the counter and added in a singsong voice, "Laura's got a boyfriend…"

"He's not my—that's just—" The oldest Hadstrom sister closed her eyes and inhaled through her nose. "You're both being ridiculous."

"Yeah, but you didn't answer my question." Nickie wiggled her eyebrows.

After a ten-second stare-down, Laura relented. "Okay. Fine. He asked if I wanted to go out for drinks tonight—"

"Ooooh." Emily wiggled her hips, and Nickie burst out laughing.

"Because I asked when he had the time to go over making a new rune for the *Gorafrex*…" Laura glared at her sisters until she couldn't hold back her smile. "And, yeah, I guess I want to see him again."

"You guess."

"Maybe, Nickie. I don't know. But if we have a reason to go out and celebrate your *record deal*…" Laura grabbed her sister by the shoulders and gave her an excited shake. Nickie let herself be jerked around, her head bobbing back and forth. She smiled. "Then maybe *I* won't feel so nervous about going out with Nathan. At night. For something that sounds way more like a date than walking to lunch from his office."

Emily looked up from her cutting board and stared out the window over the sink into the backyard. "Hey, that *does* sound serious…"

"Oh, cut it out, Em." Laura couldn't help smiling, and the flush rising in her cheeks wasn't as bad as it got around

Nathan. "So...do we wanna go out tonight before we get back to breaking ancient machinery tomorrow?"

"I feel like we already had this conversation." Emily turned around to face the table. "Me and John. Going out. Tonight. *Alone.*"

Laura blew her a raspberry. "That's right."

"Don't worry. You'll get to that point eventually. It's something you don't see every day, though." Emily smirked and tipped her chef's knife sideways.

"What?"

"Your big sister begging for chaperones on her first date since eighth grade school dance."

Nickie burst into laughter, leaning over the table and shaking her head. Laura's mouth opened in surprise and a little amusement. She couldn't think of anything to say to that. Emily shot her a wink and turned to face the counter.

"At least I can count on you to tell me how you really feel, Em."

"I got your back. Every day of the week." Emily shrugged. "Except tonight."

Nickie jumped in her chair at the unexpected buzzing of her phone in her back pocket. She pulled it out and found the text from Chuck she'd been waiting to get. "Okay, I gotta go. Meeting Chuck for lunch, then we're heading to Dave's office." She took a deep breath and stood. "Wish me luck."

"All the luck in the world!" Emily brandished her knife at her sister and waved it like she used to wave her wand before their legacy rings took care of spellcasting logistics. Then she noticed what she was doing and cracked herself up all over again.

"You'll do great." Laura smiled and gave Nickie a reassuring nod. "You always do. The Queen of Blues gets what she wants." She pointed at her sister, and Nickie pointed right back.

"I'm gonna give Chuck all the credit for this one. And I'll tell him you said something about how amazing he is at his job."

Laura chuckled. "Hey, if anything happens, just send me a 9-1-1 text, huh? I'll show up and surprise the crap outta Dave. Claim family emergency and get you out."

"Huh." Nickie tilted her head in consideration. "Any chance you wanna sit downstairs in the lobby, just in case?"

"Not really, no."

They laughed, and Nickie stuck her phone in her pocket. "Worth a shot. Okay. I'll see you guys later." She didn't even wait for a response but whirled around and power-walked through the kitchen. When she bent over to tug her boots on, she kept swiping her massive amounts of thick hair away so she could see. Finally, she straightened, tossed her hair, and pulled her shoulders back. She nodded at the door and left the house.

"So…" Emily leaned against the counter and stared at the front door a few seconds. "That was a weird moment of Nickie embodying the worst parts of both of us."

Laura chuckled. "Definitely not the worst. But yeah, I haven't seen her that frazzled in a while."

"Did you just use the word 'frazzled'?"

"I did, Em. I have an extensive vocabulary, and I'm not afraid to use it."

With a snort, Emily turned back and combined the separate parts of the salad into a giant green bowl their mom had given them when they'd first moved into the house on Pressler Street. "Well, I promise you your extensive vocabulary never made you salad like this." She grabbed plates and forks and brought everything to the table.

"No, that's definitely you." Laura helped her set the table and peered over the edge of the salad bowl. "You're my favorite chef ever."

Emily rolled her eyes and sat. "You don't get out enough for that to mean much, but thanks."

They laughed until a low whine came from the mudroom. Speed walked into the kitchen, the tags on his collar lacking their telltale jingle. His paws didn't even click across the floor before he slumped to the linoleum and splayed all four legs like he was trying to hug the floor. A grunt escaped him, following by a snorting sigh as he dropped his chin to the ground and stared at them with drooping, immortal-bulldog eyes.

Emily grimaced. "You doin' okay, there, buddy?"

Speed blinked.

"Did you take him to the vet this morning?"

"Did I—" Emily frowned at her sister and cocked her head. "Okay, if he was a normal dog, then yes, I would've dropped everything to go get his stomach pumped or whatever they do when dogs eat that much chocolate." She extended an arm toward their long-time family pet and leaned over the table. "He literally doesn't die. That's the definition of immortal. I seriously doubt that those are the first chocolate cupcakes he's eaten since, well, since chocolate and cupcakes were invented, probably."

"True." Laura peered at the bulldog staring at them and gave him a sympathetic frown. "But he looks miserable."

"Doesn't he always?" Emily grabbed a piece of chicken off her plate and held it down by the side of her chair. "Are you just tired of kibbles, buddy?" Speed rolled his eyes to look at Emily. The second he saw the chicken at eye level, he grunted his way to his feet and took it from her hand. "Hey. See?" Emily grinned at her sister and ruffled the short hair on the top of the bulldog's chubby, wrinkly head. "He's fine. You're such a drama queen, dog." As if he'd had enough, the bulldog licked his muzzle and shuffled through the kitchen and the mudroom into the living room on the other side of the house.

"I don't know..." Laura watched him with narrowed eyes. "He *is* a dog. What do you think all those cupcakes did to him if they can't, you know, kill him?"

"I think the right question is what *didn't* they...aw, *man*..." Emily's fork clattered to the plate, and she flung her arm over the back of the chair to glare into the living room. "Dude! Not in the kitchen. Come *on*."

Laura's nostrils flared, and she grimaced at her sister before giving in and plugging her nose with her fingers. "Was that the cupcakes?"

Emily waved her hand in front of her face and coughed. "If it is, that dog's been eating cupcakes and chocolate frosting for thousands of years and nobody ever knew about it." They sat there in disgust until the stench disappeared.

Emily nodded at her sister's plate. "You better still eat that."

CHAPTER SEVENTEEN

Chuck laughed as he and Nickie stepped off the sidewalk on Colorado Street toward the office building's front doors. "Okay, babe. Tone it down on the nervous smile, huh?"

"What nervous smile?" Nickie peeled her lips back to expose all her teeth in more of a silent snarl.

Her boyfriend snorted and pulled the door open. "Sure, pretend like you don't know what I'm talking about. I've never seen you this—"

"This what?" Chuck held the door open for her and they entered the lobby. "What do I look like right now?" Just to mess with him, she widened her eyes and forced herself not to blink.

"Honestly, you look like you're about to be put on trial for murder or something. This is a *good* meeting, remember?" He wrapped his arm around her and pulled her close for a sideways hug. "This is all about you being awesome, Nickie. About being the best at what you do. Man." With a quick glance at the ceiling, he blinked and shook his head. "And I seriously mean *the best*."

"Well, you're the guy who set this whole thing up, so I guess I just have to take your word for it." She grinned at him as they stopped in front of the elevators and pressed the call button.

"I wouldn't have been able to do that if you hadn't been rocking Austin's socks off for the last six months."

"Eight, actually. I think."

Chuck smiled, drew her toward him, and planted a hard kiss on her lips. "See? You're running the show, babe. I'm just making sure everything in the background does what it needs to do so you can blow us all away."

Smiling, Nickie rested her head on his shoulder and slipped her arm around his waist. *I need to blow that escaped witch-killer away. That's what I need to do.* After *this meeting.* The elevator doors opened, and they stepped inside. She turned to reach for the floor buttons and paused. "Which one is it, again?"

"Seven."

The number seven lit up under her finger, and as the doors closed, she stared at the screen counting up the floors. Chuck slipped his fingers through hers and gave them a little squeeze. "You already know Dave. You already know he wants to sign you. That's what we're here for. Nothing's gonna mess that up, got it?"

Nickie raised her eyebrows. "You know, I like the way you pep-talk. Can I sign you on as my personal cheer-leader, too?"

He cupped her cheek. "Naw. That's free." He kissed her

again, slow and passionate and the exact opposite of the one from seven floors below. Nickie let herself breathe him in, and then she let go of being nervous because she just didn't have room to hold onto that *and* grab two fistfuls of Chuck's hair. His back thumped against the wall of the elevator, his hands slipping up the back of her t-shirt. The ding and whispering hush of the elevator doors sliding open stopped them from doing more.

Nickie let out a low laugh and bit his bottom lip. "I'm feeling much better."

Chuck glanced at the ceiling of the elevator and cocked his head. "Yeah, but now I'm not thinking about meetings. Definitely not about Dave. Aw…" He mocked pouting and hunched his shoulders. "Now I just ruined it."

She pulled him by the hand from the elevator and smoothed down the pieces of his short blonde hair. "Business time for the meeting. And business time again after, huh?"

When she winked at him, Chuck's eyes grew wide, and he glanced over his shoulder at the empty hallway into the lobby of Blue Silk Records. "You know how confusing it is when you use the same phrase for two *completely* different things?"

Nickie stuck her tongue out a little through her grin. "I think you can figure it out."

Her boyfriend pressed his lips together and cocked his head, fighting with himself to get his head back into the game and not somewhere else. "Are you blackmailing me into *making* Dave sign you?"

"Hey, that is *not* blackmail." She shook her hair out of

her eyes and shrugged. "That was a thank you for getting me this far. And I'll thank you again later."

"Yeah, no pressure or anything." They both laughed and headed into the lobby toward a huge front desk against the back wall.

"Nickie!" The woman behind the desk, wearing a shimmering silver pantsuit, her hair done up in an elaborate bun on top of her head, leaned over the desk and waved. "Good to see you."

"Hey, Charlie." Nickie nodded with an enthusiastic smile. "How's it goin'?"

"Just another Tuesday. Just got better, though. Dave went on and on yesterday about setting up this meeting. I can't imagine why."

Nickie chuckled and held up crossed fingers.

"Is he in his office?" Chuck asked, grabbing Nickie's hand and peering down the hall.

"Yep. Been in there since he came in. He's probably getting ready." Charlie gave them a sweet smile and nodded toward the hallway. "Good luck."

"This woman doesn't need luck." Chuck reached around Nickie's back and pointed at the top of her head. "She *is* luck."

Nickie shot him an amused glance as Charlie laughed softly behind the desk and got back to work. "What does that even mean?"

They stepped down the hall, and Chuck hummed in consideration. "That my entire life has only gotten better since I met you."

"Hey, good answer."

"Yeah, I know."

They stopped in front of Dave's office, and Chuck paused before opening the door.

Good thing the blinds are down. Just a few more seconds for me to step into my big-artist shoes. Breathe.

"This is just the beginning, babe." Chuck nodded and took a deep breath. "You ready?"

"I'm ready. Yeah, I'm ready." She laughed and nudged his arm. "Quit asking me that and just open the door."

He grinned and grabbed the doorknob. "Here we go."

The door swung into Dave's office, which Nickie had only seen once before. She recognized Blue Silk Records' logo on the left wall, blown to massive proportions, a shimmering blue piece of fabric that was supposed to be silk, draped off the top of the B, flowing out as if blown by the wind. A few more awards decorated the walls since the last time she was here.

"Hey, man." Chuck entered and stepped aside for Nickie to come in behind him. "Big day, right?"

Dave sat in his huge leather chair behind the desk, his face darkened a little by the bright summer sunshine drifting in through the wall of windows behind him. He had his eyes closed and seemed to be sleeping.

Chuck glanced at Nickie and snorted. "Hasn't come out all morning? Yeah, he's sleeping something off." He stepped toward the desk and rapped on it, loud and fast, with his knuckles. "Dave! This is one meeting you don't wanna sleep through."

His friend's eyes opened slowly, but the guy didn't look like he'd just woken up. He looked pissed. "Leave." Dave's voice came out low and threatening, and he glared at Chuck standing in front of him.

Chuck let out an unsure laugh. "Very funny. Come on, you've got the best blues-rock guitarist in Texas standing in your office. Let's do this, huh?" He stepped aside and opened his arm toward Nickie so the owner of Blue Silk Records got a good look at her.

Nickie grinned and lifted a hand. "Hey, Dave."

The man she'd come to sign a record deal with sat up straight in his chair and blinked at her. His expressionless face twisted into a snarl. "*You.*" A silver light flashed in his eyes, and Chuck stepped back.

Crap. No. Nickie swallowed and glanced at Chuck, who stared at his friend, baffled by a display of magic he didn't know how to explain.

"Dude, what's wrong with your eyes—"

Dave sent his chair flying backward into the wall of windows and shoved his hands toward Nickie. A thousand black, swirling bubbles erupted from his fingertips and straight for her.

She didn't have time to think of a spell or some way to keep any of this under wraps before her secrets burst open. The ring did that for her. Nickie lifted her hand, the black legacy ring on her thumb flashed twice, and every single one of the bubbles were swallowed up by a bright yellow light curving away from her fingers.

"What the hell?" Chuck shouted, glancing back and forth between the two people he thought he knew best in the world.

The Gorafrex controlling Dave's body turned on Chuck and opened his mouth in a silent scream. A massive red bubble grew between his lips and launched at Chuck.

Nickie ran forward and raised both hands. Her ring

flashed, putting the same shield around Chuck she'd just used. When the red bubble hit her yellow light, it burst into thousands of tiny round drops, whirling and buzzing through the air like countless flies. One of them made it around the magical yellow shield and a tiny bead of magic landed on Chuck's shoulder, sending him flying into the bookcase against the wall beside the giant logo.

Nickie lifted a hand at the Gorafrex and shouted, "*Sepelio!*"

A fiery red streak burst from her hand while she aimed the other at Chuck, keeping the growing version of her yellow shield around him as the air swarmed with tiny beads of blood magic.

The Gorafrex in Dave's body ducked her attack and leapt up onto the desk. He snarled at her, and as she reached to shoot off another spell—any spell that came to mind—Dave launched off the desk. He darted for the open door, barreling into the hallway, leaving a trail of crashes and surprised shouts behind him. Someone screamed, glass shattered, and Nickie didn't care one way or the other what was happening out there. The most important thing was slumped against the bookshelf.

"Chuck. No, no, no." She raced to him and fell to her knees.

He groaned, his eyes fluttering open, and caught sight of the Gorafrex's red drops of magic swirling around them. "What—" He tried to scramble back, but the bookcase stopped him.

Nickie moved the yellow glow of the shield a little farther away from them and only had to think about it opening up like it had for her a few seconds before. The yellow light curved and sucked the red drops into it and each one disappeared. She dropped her hand by her side, her shield vanished, and the office went silent.

She turned to him with wide eyes and swallowed. "Are you okay?"

"What?" Chuck blinked and shook his head. "No, Nickie." His hand went up to rub the place on his shoulder where the blood bubble struck before launching him across the room. "I can't even..." He blinked and glanced around. "What just happened?"

"Does anything hurt? Like, physically? Are you okay?" She reached toward him to search his body, and he leaned away.

"Yeah, I think *physically*, I'll manage. I don't know about the rest of me." He stared at her with wide eyes.

That's exactly the look I imagined him giving me if he ever found out about magic. This is not gonna be fun for either of us. Nickie took a deep breath. "I'm so sorry."

"Don't be sorry, Nickie. You don't ever have to apologize to me." Chuck shook his head and glanced away from her. "But whatever that was...that was something you should've told me about a long time ago."

She sat on her heels and nodded. "I know. Believe me, it's not because I didn't *want* to tell you. It's just...there are certain things I can't do."

"Not anymore." He shoved his hands against the floor and pushed himself up, then leaned against the bookcase and grunted. "Please tell me what just happened, Nickie. If I don't...if I don't get an explanation, I'm gonna think I'm crazy."

"You're not crazy." She slid her hand down his arm and

grabbed his fingers. For a few seconds, he didn't react, then he laced his fingers through hers and frowned. "Yeah, I guess it's not actually breaking any rules if you've already seen it," she said.

"Screw the rules, babe. Tell me what's going on."

Nickie took a deep breath. "Okay, first, you should know that some people would say the best way to handle this is to wipe your memory of the whole day and call it a job."

Chuck's eyes grew wide, and his nostrils flared as he stared at her. "You're not one of those people."

"No." A wry chuckle escaped her, and she bit her lip. "I don't even know how to do that, so it's not really an option."

"Good. Start talking." He squeezed her hand and stared at her.

Nickie wanted to just tell him he must've hit his head way too hard and just needed to rest. *Except that's the last thing I want. He deserves to know. Especially now.* "It's gonna sound crazy and totally impossible."

He laughed without amusement and gestured at Dave's office and the scattered papers lying everywhere after the man had jumped off his desk. "We're past that point, now. As long as what you're about to tell me is the *whole* truth, we won't have any problems."

"Chuck, I never wanted to—"

"Just please, *don't* lie to me anymore, Nickie." His other hand settled on top of hers, and she realized he was shaking. "I can handle everything else. Just not you lying to me."

"Yeah, okay." She nodded and slid closer to him on the floor. "I'm gonna start with saying magic…is real."

MARTHA CARR & MICHAEL ANDERLE

"Uh huh…"

"And…I'm a witch." She looked over her shoulder and whispered a spell to hide them from view.

Chuck stared at her but didn't say a word until she'd finished telling him everything.

CHAPTER EIGHTEEN

Laura sat on the living room couch, sipping an afternoon cup of coffee, flipping the pages of a Peabrain spellbook she'd been given by a former coworker. She'd almost reached the end, skimming for an hour, before she decided to call it.

"I shouldn't be disappointed." She closed the book and set it on the coffee table. "Humans had nothing to do with building this ship or with putting the Gorafrex in its prison. But is it too much to ask that the most powerful magical beings out of all of us know just a *little* about rune-making?" She took a long drink of coffee at just the right temperature, and with a sigh, settled back into the couch. "I hope Nathan has some information." She blinked, aware of the flaring nerves in her belly at the sound of his name. "Yeah, that's not helping."

As soon as she relaxed, the front door burst open. Laura nearly spilled her coffee all over herself. Hissing through her teeth, she set the cup on the coffee table as Nickie barreled into the house followed by a confused and worried-looking Chuck.

"Hey." Laura stood and folded her arms, grinning. "Looks like we have a signed musician in the—"

Nickie gazed at her with wide eyes and shook her head. Then, she glanced at Chuck, who stood just inside the doorway. He stared around the house like he hadn't been there hundreds of times.

"Okay…" He nodded, his expression warring between awe and confusion. "All the weird stuff here is starting to make more sense now."

"Hey, you wanna come sit down?" Nickie grabbed his hand and nodded toward the living room.

"The couch is just a couch, right?" He pointed at the item in question and peered around the corner to take in the living room.

"Yeah, babe. It's just a couch."

"I mean, it's not like I'd be able to tell, right?" A disbelieving chuckle escaped him, Nickie led him into the living room. He sat down, he giggled a little, and laid his head back on the cushion.

"You want something to drink?"

"What?"

"Babe, something to drink. Water? Beer? Coffee?"

"Definitely not coffee." He shook his head, blinking. "Is the beer…"

"The beer's fine. I'll get you a beer." Nickie turned away and passed Laura, who'd watched them, completely clueless.

"What's wrong with him?" Laura whispered when her sister walked past.

"Kitchen." Nickie disappeared into the dining room and around the corner.

Laura glanced at Chuck, who leaned over his lap and rubbed his temples. "Okay." She followed her sister into the kitchen. "Nickie, what's going on?"

"You're really not gonna like this." Nickie stood from the fridge, closed the door, and stuck both beers, one after the other, beneath the bottle opener nailed to the cabinet. She tipped one back and chugged a few mouthfuls.

"Um...what happened in that meeting?"

"Ha!" Nickie stared at her sister, opened her mouth to say something, then took another drink of beer.

"Okay, it can't be *that* bad, Nickie. Unless..." Laura stepped toward her and lowered her voice. "Did you hear the drums?"

"The *drums*. No, I didn't hear the drums. But I *did* find the Gorafrex's new host."

"Hey, that's good."

"It's Dave."

"Dave? Chuck's..." Laura pointed toward the other side of the house, and Nickie nodded. "Oh, my god."

"Yeah. We walked into his office to sign this deal and that *thing* was inside him, Laura. It attacked me and could've hurt Chuck *way* worse than a little toss against a bookshelf." Nickie leaned back against the fridge and drank until her bottle was nearly empty.

"Did Chuck see it?"

"He saw everything." Nickie shrugged. "He didn't exactly freak out, but it's not like he sees stuff like that every day."

"What did you tell him?"

"Everything."

"Everything? We can't tell humans everything. You *know* that—"

"What was I supposed to do, huh? He saw it *all*. It's not like I have any idea how to wipe away memories, and he didn't just see it as a random pedestrian walking by a car crash or something. The Gorafrex is using his friend, and it attacked us, and Chuck deserves to know what's going on. That's the least I can do after ripping apart his entire life and everything he thought he knew."

Laura nodded and glanced through the mudroom, though she couldn't quite see Chuck from where she stood. "Yeah, he does deserve to know. Wow. I'm sorry he had to find out like that."

"Yeah, you and me both." Nickie bit her lip and stared at the wall across from the fridge. Her eyes and nose started tingled with the first wave of tears, but she pushed it back and stood straight. "The Gorafrex got away." She couldn't look at her sister and the disappointed expression she knew she'd find there.

"What?"

"I tried to stop it." Nickie shrugged. "I'm not exactly the best at attack spells. You know that."

"Hey, look at me." Laura stepped closer and waited for Nickie to meet her gaze. "I would *never* expect you to take that thing down by yourself. Are you kidding me? It's not even possible. We're still looking for the last part of what we need to put it away, and it's something the three of us have to do together. So don't apologize. That was the right decision, because you're safe. And so is Chuck." They both leaned to glance around the corner, where Chuck had both arms over the back of the couch and his head bent back against the cushion, blowing raspberries at the ceiling. "Mostly."

"He's safe. We'll make sure of that." Nickie headed through the mudroom and turned to whisper, "So far, he's taken it pretty well, but there's gonna be some adjustment time, right? So just go easy on him. Please."

Laura nodded and followed her sister to the living room.

Nickie stepped around the couch with a reassuring smile and handed the beer bottle to her boyfriend. "This might help. A little." When he took it from her, she glanced at Laura and gave her a look that said her sister needed to help her out. Nickie sat next to the baffled Chuck.

Laura took a deep breath and headed for the armchair on the other side of the coffee table. "So…" With a smile, she sat and nodded. "Rough day, huh?"

He looked at Nickie, then turned his attention to Laura. "You don't have to rub it in, you know."

Laura bit her lip. "Sorry. If it helps at all, this is the first time we've ever…um…" She pursed her lips, trying to find the right words. "We've never had to explain anything to anyone before, so it's kinda new for us too."

"Yeah, that doesn't really help. But thanks." Chuck lifted his beer toward her before taking a long drink. He blew out a sigh and stared at the coffee table. "Let me recap this, okay?"

Nickie glanced over at her sister.

Shrugging, Laura added, "Okay."

"Magic is a thing. Planet Earth isn't a planet but a spaceship that got lost in space."

"Actually, it's not so much *lost* as it was thrown off—"

"*Laura.*" Nickie shook her head, and her sister pressed her lips together.

"You, Laura, and Emily are witches, which is like another race that comes from a different planet." Chuck scratched his head. "Boy, you know, I've always believed in aliens, but this is *not* the way I expected to…."

"We're not aliens like *that.*" Laura glanced around the room, hoping she could come up with something helpful. "I mean, all of these races have been on the ship since it left Arenya V thousands of years ago. We're from Earth just as much as you are."

He cocked his head. "*All* of these races?" He frowned at Nickie. "There are more? You didn't mention anything but witches and wizards and humans."

"Yeah, that's because that's all we're dealing with right now. In our lives, most of the time." Nickie rubbed his back and hoped some of this would help him not freak out. "There are a lot of different races, it's true. I just didn't want to overwhelm you with mentioning every one of them, which you probably won't even see, so it's not an issue."

"Unless I've already seen them and just didn't know it." Chuck rubbed his chin. "This is nuts."

"Well, let's just stick with the basics for now, okay?" Nickie shot her sister another warning glance. Laura did a relatively good job of not trying to overexplain a complicated rule that was sure to fry Chuck's brain, so the three of them just sat in silence.

Chuck took a sharp, sudden breath and turned to Nickie. "And that thing you guys are trying to…lock up."

"The Gorafrex, yeah." Laura nodded and forced herself not to keep going.

"Yeah. Gorafrex. It kills people?"

"Just witches and wizards, actually." Nickie shifted uncomfortably on the couch and tried not to jump up and run away to hide in a dark closet somewhere. *This is the weirdest conversation, especially because it's Chuck.*

Her boyfriend frowned. "So, it's like a dietary thing?"

"Not..." Nickie almost laughed. "More like it needs witch and wizard magic to sustain itself. I mean, I guess that *might* fall under dietary."

"And it took over Dave's body."

The Hadstrom sisters exchanged a glance and took a few seconds to respond. "Pretty much," Nickie said. "But Dave's fine. He's still in there, and that thing can't hurt him. It's probably scary, yeah, but Dave won't remember anything once it's gone."

"So...it *will* leave."

"Definitely."

Chuck glanced from one sister to the other. "What's gonna happen to him after that?"

"That's just..." Laura bit her lip and glanced at Nickie.

"That's something only Dave gets to find out, really." The middle Hadstrom sister shrugged and drank her beer. *There's only so much we can tell him. The fact that humans have a second brain and the most powerful magic out of all of us is not on that list. Not today while the Gorafrex is running around waking up those brains and dropping hosts into a new world of chaos.*

CHAPTER NINETEEN

"Man." Chuck shook his head, drank some more beer, and leaned forward over his knees. "Why Dave, though?"

"No idea," Laura said. "We haven't even figured out yet if that part's random or not. He didn't *do* anything, Chuck. That's the part that really sucks about this. As far as we know, it's random, and none of us can predict who's next or when or how."

"Except now that thing knows a lot more about us than it did before." Nickie rubbed the back of her neck and pushed back into the couch cushions.

"You mean that we know Dave?" Chuck asked. "Wait, you guys didn't actually know any of the other people, did you?"

"The other hosts?"

"'People' sounds a lot less creepy, Laura." He raised his beer toward her.

"Okay. Well, I'm guessing that it at least made the

connection between the two of you and Dave," Laura offered.

"I'm not talking about that, though." Nickie shifted away from Chuck to look him in the eyes. "Charlie said Dave had been in his office all morning. I think he came in with the Gorafrex already there."

"Why would that thing pretend to be Dave for half a day?"

"I don't know. Maybe it takes some getting used to. But if it *was* using Dave for that long before we got there…" Nickie frowned. "It knew where to go. It knew where Dave worked, and which office was his…it might know exactly who we are now."

"Oh, great." Laura closed her eyes.

"I don't…I don't get it." Chuck glanced back and forth between them. "Why is that bad if it knows you're witches?"

"That's not the problem, babe." Nickie put a sympathetic hand on his shoulder. "The Gorafrex can tell who's human and who's anything else. It's a problem for us because we've run into that thing a few times trying to stop it."

"Didn't work." Laura shook her head.

"If that thing can read Dave's memories, it knows everything about us Dave knows. Our names. That we're all Hadstroms, in case the thing had any doubt about us being the ones coming for it. It knows where we live and who our friends are. I don't know how much you and Dave have talked about our lives." Nickie gestured to her sister and then herself. "Whatever he knows, though, it'll use against us."

Laura rubbed her forehead and stood from the armchair. "That means we can't waste any more time with this extra stuff. We need to tear down the rest of those energy cores, pronto. At least one to keep the escape pod from fully powering, but as many as we can if we don't want magic to get any worse."

"Oh, it's getting worse." Chuck nodded, like he knew what they were talking about. "Was it bad to begin with?"

"Yesterday morning, at least." Nickie wrinkled her nose. "There were a few weird things happening."

"And they keep getting weirder," Laura added. "And probably more dangerous, the longer this goes on." She turned toward the staircase off the foyer, then stopped. "Oh..."

"What's wrong?"

"Emily already left."

Nickie leaned forward on the couch. "How is she gone already? It's only..." She pulled her phone out of her back pocket to check the time. "Oh. Wow, really? How did it get to six o'clock so fast?"

"Well, how much time did you spend filling Chuck in on all the...stuff?"

"The stuff." Chuck snorted. "That sums it up."

"I guess longer than I thought." Nickie offered a tiny smile. "That was worth it, though. You needed to know everything."

Her boyfriend cleared his throat and nodded at his beer. "Honestly, I can't say what's worth it and what isn't. I'm just gonna let this all sink in and hope I don't end up in some mental institution."

"That won't happen." When he looked at Nickie, she

saw he truly believed her, which was the only thing keeping either of them sane through all this.

"Well, Chuck, I guess you're in luck. Make yourself at home while everything sinks in." Laura clapped her hands together and caught her sister's gaze. "We should go."

"Wait, what?" Chuck blinked at them both with those blue puppy-dog eyes Nickie had fallen in love with, and it killed her that she had to agree with her sister.

"Sorry, babe." She stood, bent down to cup his cheeks, and kissed him. "This is one of those time-sensitive sister things, you know? Where we run off to do something after giving you a super weird and confusing explanation. Only this time, you know where we're going."

"No I don't." The man sat there, unable to decide which one of the Hadstrom sisters he wanted to plead with more. "Where are you going?"

Nickie stuck her phone into her pocket and nodded, more to reassure herself than anything. "You know. Go tear down an ancient and highly sophisticated piece of Velikan technology so a bloodthirsty creature without its own body won't power an escape pod and blast a hole through all of Austin. And the world." His mouth dropped open, and she just raised her eyebrows. "Sorry. Was that too much?"

Chuck's voice broke when he said, "A little."

"I promise we'll be back in about an hour and a half, two hours tops." Nickie turned toward her sister. "So, we're gonna do this without Em?"

"I mean, she made it clear she wasn't putting her date on hold for anything. Honestly, I'd feel bad about ruining her night with something like this."

Nickie snorted. "Yeah. We'll just ruin her day tomorrow. Speed!" Nickie leaned toward the mudroom and whistled through her teeth. The click of their bulldog's paws across the floor came from the upstairs hallways instead. It took the family pet a good minute to shuffle his chubby self down the stairs, then he trotted into the living room, wagging his tail while his tongue hung from one side of his mouth. Nickie squatted to scratch behind his ears and pointed at Chuck. "Just hang out with him for a while, okay? He could use a little company right now."

"Actually, yeah." Chuck let out a small laugh that didn't sound like he was about to lose it. The bulldog hopped onto the couch beside him, reveling in the huge amount of attention he was about to get. "I like you, Speed. Just another normal guy in this weird world. That's what I need right now. A regular dog with regular-dog instincts and..." When he looked at the Hadstrom sisters standing in the foyer, his stomach dropped. "Wait. He...he *is* just a regular dog, right?" His hand lifted from Speed's back, and the bulldog nuzzled his wrist to keep going.

Nickie licked her lips. "Not really."

Speed grunted, and Chuck flinched away for a second before settling his hand back down on the dog's back. "I'm gonna pretend I didn't hear that. We're good, buddy."

Laura grabbed her keys. "Uh..." She lowered her voice and leaned toward her sister. "Do we still need to hide things, or..."

"I mean, there's no point now, right?"

"Go ahead," Chuck called, leaning back against the couch again with his eyes closed as he petted their immortal bulldog. "I doubt anything can surprise me at this point."

Nickie almost bursting out laughing, but she held it together. "Go for it."

"'Kay." Laura thumbed her keyring and disappeared from the living room with a little pop.

Chuck opened his eyes and rolled his head toward Nickie. "Do I get to see any—where's Laura?"

Nickie looked up at the ceiling and hummed. "She'll be right—"

Laura popped out of the Clubhouse and right back to where she'd been standing.

"Jeeze." Chuck sat upright and stared at her. "What *is* that thing?"

Laura patted the Velikan wrench slung over her shoulder. "This is an incredibly powerful weapon used to deactivate—"

"One of the giants who designed this ship gave Laura a super-sized wrench to hit things with." Nickie stuck her thumb at her sister and grinned.

Chuck barked out a laugh and leaned back against the couch. "There are totally still mundane things in the world of magical…things." Nickie smirked at her sister and folded her arms. "You have no idea."

"All right, let's leave the cutting remarks, huh?" Laura nodded at the legacy ring on her sister's hand.

When Nickie raised her hand a little, her black ring flashed and produced another iridescent transport bubble. Just before it grew large enough for them to step inside, Chuck opened his mouth to say something, but the words never came when he saw his girlfriend and her sister step into a giant bubble appearing out of nowhere.

"Let's do the next one by the golf course," Laura muttered.

"Got it." Nickie caught Chuck staring. She blew him a kiss and winked before the bubble and the Hadstrom sisters vanished.

Chuck choked and couldn't think of anything to do but sit there and keep petting the witches' bulldog. "Okay. Just gonna let things sink in. That's easy enough, right?"

Speed licked his chops and rolled his eyes before the sound and the stench of the dog's perpetual gastro-intestinal plague hit Chuck full force.

"You need to get that checked." Chuck covered his nose and swallowed. "Any other day, buddy, I'd be running out of this room. Just this once, though, I'll let it go." He coughed and pulled his shirt up over his nose. "If I don't pass out first."

CHAPTER TWENTY

"This is...really nice." Emily swept her gaze over the inside of Creekside Bistro and took a small sip of the wine John had ordered them.

"Yeah?" Her date grinned at her and eyed the mostly full dining room. "There aren't a lot of places that fit my standards for taking you out, but this one's been a favorite for a while. Never anything less than perfect."

She smiled over the rim of her wineglass. "But does it stand up to Meadowlark?"

"Um... right now, I'd say the restaurant we both work for has fallen a little in the ranks of Austin's best fine dining."

"Oh." Emily sighed and glanced down at the table. "You know, I haven't been back at work since I left Sunday. I'd completely forgotten about that whole... weird issue."

"Seriously?" John smiled, but he looked way too confused for Emily's liking. "I mean, it's kinda hard to forget. Two different days in just over a week where all the customers start freaking out and acting like…I don't know. Like they never learned how to be adults."

"Yeah, I know. It's been weird." *And it would be even weirder if he knew I'm the reason everyone lost it. I really gotta learn to separate work and everything else. Especially the magical everything else.* "I guess I've had a lot going on since Sunday."

"Not a very relaxing two days off, huh?"

She chuckled. "Not really."

"Well, I promised you we'd have fun tonight, so that's what we're gonna do." John lifted his wineglass, Emily clinked hers against it, and they drank. "This is just the dinner part, by the way."

"No way." Emily slapped her hand against her cheek in mock surprise. "In a restaurant?"

"I know. It's shocking." John leaned forward over the table and wiggled his eyebrows. "But after we eat, we're going somewhere else."

"Oh, *that's* the surprise."

"Now you're catching on."

"Perfect. I like surprises." She felt her cheeks growing warm with what little wine she'd already had. *As long as they're happy surprises where nobody gets possessed or kidnapped or murdered to power an escape pod. There's a wide range, there.* Her knee started bouncing up and down under the table.

"How's Nickie doing?"

"What?" Emily blinked and looked up at him again.

"Your sister. She's still your sister, right?"

"Yeah…are you *sure* you're not pulling out all these surprises for me just so you can get to know my sister?"

John's mouth twitched as he tried to determine whether she was joking. "Yeah, I'm sure. I was talking about the party Sunday night. You know, when you and your sisters ran out and spent the rest of the night looking for her migraine medicine?"

Emily's eyes widened, and she covered her mouth with her hand to keep from laughing. "Oh. Yeah, *that.*"

"Wow, you really have had a busy few days off."

"Trust me, we could sit here all night and I probably wouldn't even cover half of it." *I need to stop talking.* "Nickie's fine. Those migraine pills are...hard to find. We went to a couple different places before a pharmacy finally had some. She's stocked up for a while now, I think." *All lies, Emily. Nickie really undersold how hard it is to cover up all this 'being a witch and dating a human' stuff.*

"I'm glad she's okay. She didn't look good."

"Yeah, when she gets hit, she gets hit hard. But you still hung out at the party for a while after?"

John nodded and sipped his wine. "Chuck's pretty cool. I mean, at least he was able to explain to Nathan and me that leaving parties right when they start to get good is just something you and your sisters do."

"Oh, man. It sounds awful when you say it like that." Emily took a deep breath and glanced around the dining room. "It's not something that we *try* to do. We're just... really close. Sometimes things come up we have to help each other with."

"Yeah, I get that. I mean, I can imagine what it's like. I don't have two sisters, so it's not the same."

"Right." She stared at him a few seconds and grew a little restless. *What my sisters and I have going on right now is anything but normal, trust me.* Her knee bounced faster under the table, and she stared at the white tablecloth between her and John. *You need to chill out, Em. Calm down. Don't get worked up. This is a date. With John. Who you really like.*

"You okay?" John raised an eyebrow and cocked his head.

"Yeah, I'm okay." She nodded. "Why wouldn't I be?"

"You're kind of...trembling?" An unsure laugh escaped him. "I didn't mean to push about Nickie or anything."

"No, no. You weren't pushing. It's fine. I'm fine." Emily tapped her thigh beneath the table and used the same spell she'd cast at her college graduation when her fidgety body wouldn't do what she wanted. Immediately, her leg fell still under the immobility charm, and she grinned. "So, in case you couldn't tell, I really needed a night out without my sisters."

He laughed and raised his glass. "Here's to dates where nobody else tags along." Emily rolled her eyes but tipped her wineglass against his anyway. *And let's hope we didn't just jinx the night with that.* As soon as she took another sip of wine to end John's toast, her other leg started twitching. "Oh, jeeze." She clamped her other hand down on the second rebel limb.

"What's wrong?"

"It's fine. Sometimes I just get...muscle cramps? I think." *You sound like a crazy person, Emily.*

John chuckled and tried to lick the smirk off his face. "I might be able to help."

"Uh...probably not. I mean, nothing against you, but the stuff I'm dealing with right now is kind of..." Emily wrinkled her nose. "Unusual. Abnormal. Off the charts, maybe. I don't know the terms."

"Oh, man. I didn't actually tell you, did I?"

"Tell me what?" Her heart leapt into her throat as she tried to anticipate what he could possibly tell her that could help her in any way. *Keep it together, Em...* A silver flash caught her eye on the table in front of John. The knife beside his plate trembled. *No.*

John took another drink and smiled. "I'm going to school part time for Massage Therapy. So I probably *could* help. At least a little."

Her eyes whipped up to meet his gaze, and she gulped. "What?"

"Okay, I know that sounds weird from a guy you just started dating, but I promise it's actually true."

The knife jerked sideways. Emily tried to stare it down as hard as she could. *If this is some weird kinda new magic coming out to play, I don't want it. Not now.*

"Okay." John wrinkled his nose and stared at her. "I just made this weird by telling you that, didn't I?"

"Huh?" She looked up at him and felt like a complete idiot.

"I'm sorry, Em. I normally don't tell people, but I just... you're obviously distracted by something. Maybe it's muscle cramps or something else. I don't know. I was just trying to help." He set his glass down on the table and shrugged.

"No, you didn't do anything wrong." The words came out of her in a rush. "I'm trying to get my—" The wiggling knife flung itself from where it was supposed to stay next to John's plate and clanged against the stem of the wineglass. Both glass and wine toppled over onto the tablecloth and all over John's button-down shirt.

Emily squeaked and clamped her hands over her mouth.

John spread his arms and stared at the mess Emily's wayward magic had made.

"Oh, my god. John. I'm so sorry." She stood from the booth, snatched her napkin, and tried to sop up what hadn't yet soaked into anything else.

He frowned at her above an unsettled smile. "Why are *you* sorry?"

"Um…" She glanced at the spill and up at him. "Mostly because I didn't want to make you feel bad about anything you tell me. Ever. I know I didn't knock over your wine glass. Duh." She rolled her eyes and giggled, but it didn't feel anywhere close to convincing.

"Uh…no." With a raised eyebrow, John eyed her then glanced at the wine-soaked front of his shirt. "All right." He grabbed his napkin and pressed it against his chest and upper stomach, then just left it there. "Now neither one of us have to look at it."

Emily snorted and sat again. *I can't believe this is happening now. Right now. Why?* "At least it's not red."

John laughed and nodded, picking up the wineglass. "Yeah. At least there's that. Still weird, though." He gave the wineglass stem an experimental tug and frowned. "Nothing wrong with the glass. Did I…" Once he'd scanned the tabletop and found nothing there, his frown deepened. "Didn't set it on anything. That's just weird."

"So weird." Emily offered a little shrug. "Do you want another drink?"

"Yeah, I'll get it when our server comes back. So, we were talking about—"

"You going to school for Massage Therapy." Emily sat up straight in the booth and nodded. "I think it's awesome."

"Oh, yeah? You seemed a little weirded out." He ran a hand through his brown hair and cocked his head. "And now you don't."

"No. I'm sorry. I'm..." She sighed and lowered both hands into her lap. "Just trying to decompress from the last couple days, I think. Turns out those have been more stressful than long days at work."

"Hey, it happens."

"But thanks for telling me about going to school. You know, if you don't normally tell people."

John grinned. "Well, I noticed when I do, people think I'm coming onto them or they ask to be a guinea pig while I'm still *learning* so they don't have to pay for a massage."

Emily shook her head. "Freeloaders."

"Right? By the way, the offer stands, if you still want me to see what I can do for your muscle cramps. I definitely won't charge *you*."

She played with the stem of her own wineglass and tried not to smile. "Free massage, huh? It does kinda sound like a pickup line."

"It might be." He smiled at her and his gaze lingered. "Just for you, though."

"I'm flattered." *Maybe that is what I need. Just regular relaxing things.*

"All right." Their server stopped at the table with two plates and set Emily's down in front of her first.

"Man, that smells good." John eyed Emily's plate and nodded at her. "Good choice."

"I know." She stared at her food. *This isn't what I ordered, is it? What did I even order? I can't...I hate figs.*

The server started to set John's plate in front of him but noticed the look on Emily's face. "Is everything okay?"

"Yeah." Emily swallowed. *I can't eat this. Me. The chef.* "Yeah, I'll just—"

A tiny spark flared from the middle of the pasta on John's plate and tossed almost half of the noodles—cream sauce and all—off the plate and into his lap. The server jumped in surprise, the plate slipped from her hand, and John was covered now in wine *and* pasta.

He sucked in a breath and flung the noodles off his arms and onto the table. "Yeah, that's hot."

Emily wanted to slide off the booth and under the table and disappear. *What is going on?*

"Sir, I am *so* sorry." The server gaped at him. "I don't know what—" She grabbed the plate and started scooping the slippery, well-sauced noodles onto the dish. "That shouldn't have happened."

John cracked up laughing and grabbed a huge handful of noodles. Most of them slopped back onto the table. "It's totally okay. I work front of house at Meadowlark Tavern." The young woman jerked her head up and looked terrified. "And by that I only mean that I get it when accidents happen. Weird accidents. Messy." He pulled a long noodle off his shirt and set it on the top of the pile. "I'm not gonna complain to anyone about it. Don't worry."

"I..." The server glanced at Emily, who managed to smile and not make it look like she was freaking out. At least, the smile felt better on her own face than the rest of her felt. "I'll have the kitchen make another plate for you. And it's on me."

"Actually…" John glanced at Emily, narrowed his eyes, and took a deep breath. "We'll just take the check."

"I understand." The woman grabbed the plate of upturned noodles with both hands and turned toward the kitchen.

"You're not gonna eat that, are you?"

Emily glanced at the food in front of her and swallowed. "Probably not."

"Yeah, I saw it on your face." John leaned forward to grab her napkin and tried as best he could to clean up the sauce all over his shirt. "Plus, I'm pretty sure that's not what you ordered."

"You have no idea how much better that makes me feel."

"Please don't tell me that's the nicest thing I've ever said to you."

"Ha! Not even close. I was starting to think I was going crazy. I'm really glad I'm not."

"Yeah, me too, Em." John stood from the booth and pulled a whole new pile of noodles off his pants before setting them down on the table. "And here I was going on and on about how awesome this place is."

"Everybody has bad days." She shrugged. "Some more than others." Her copper ring flashed to undo the immobility charm on her leg, and she stood.

"No kidding." Glancing over his shoulder toward the kitchen, he pulled out his wallet and rifled through it before placing four twenties on the table. "Let's go before she comes back."

Emily stared at the money. "That's way more than it costs to not eat dinner here."

He laughed. "We drank most of the wine, and I'm pretty sure that she thinks her night can't get any worse. I can make it a little better than the worst night she's ever had."

She blinked. "You're an incredible person."

"Uh…no. I just feel really bad. And I'm covered in… everything." He brushed at his shirt and gave up. "I have extra clothes in my car. That's my real motivation. Plus, I did *really* well on Sunday with tips."

"Even with all the craziness?" Emily walked beside him through the dining room, trying not to let her imagination run wild and convince her that everyone here was staring at them.

"Both of those crazy nights, actually. The first time with a bunch of anarchists in the dining room." She snorted. "And Sunday after the whatever party."

"I think they're calling it a swinger party. At least on the news." They walked past a six-top who'd just gotten their drinks and bread.

"You saw that bit too?"

"Yeah. It was really weird." *And my fault because I was too busy thinking about my little crush on John instead of focusing on the line. Most dangerous pot of soup ever created.*

John grabbed her hand. "You know, a lot of weird things have happened since I met you."

"What?" She glanced away from the six-top and stared at John. At the same instant, there was a loud *flap* of heavy fabric, followed by the crash of shattering glass and the startled shouts of diners.

"Woah." When John turned around, so did Emily.

Everyone seated at the six-top were now standing, half of them covered in drinks, breadcrumbs, and splattered buttered. The other half gaped at the mess. The tablecloth lay on the floor beneath their spilled glasses and serving plates and all their silverware. One man picked a sprig of baby's breath—which had been part of the centerpiece a few seconds before—from the hair of the woman next to him and stared at it.

"Really weird stuff," John muttered.

"What does that have to do with me?" The only thing Emily wanted to do was bolt out of the restaurant and run all the way home. *It's like ten blocks. Maybe. I can do it.*

"Nothing." John shook his head and grabbed her hand again. "Let's get outta here, huh?"

Just before they made it to the front doors, someone gasped. Emily peered back to see their server standing in front of the mess at the six-top, and the poor woman looked like she was about to cry. *This is not the night I needed it to be.* Emily followed John out of the restaurant and hoped that would take all the flying food and overreacting centerpieces out of the equation for everyone else.

CHAPTER TWENTY-ONE

"This keeps getting easier every time." Nickie watched the last few shards of the energy core rain onto the chamber floor after most of it had already crashed to the ground. The metal cradle where the glass column connected to the floor sparked with electric-green light, hissing every few seconds.

"Or maybe it has something to do with the fact that you just unleashed all your pent-up rage on part of an ancient escape pod." Laura shrugged.

"Yeah, maybe." Nickie hefted the massive Velikan socket wrench and offered it to her sister. "Thanks for letting me take a few swings."

Laura took the wrench, and her sister dusted off her hands. "No problem. You looked like you could use it."

"Guess I did."

Laura stared at Nickie under the soft glow of the glowing orb floating in the air beside them. "You wanna talk about it?"

Nickie laughed. "Here?"

"It's not like anyone's gonna barge in on us, right?"

"True. Okay." Nickie took a deep breath. "I hate that I feel so *relieved* now that Chuck knows about everything. I've been lying to him for years, and I guess I just never realized how much it was affecting me until I didn't have to lie anymore. But, I can tell he's pissed."

Laura folded her arms. "I'd call it more of a mind-explosion."

"Come on." Nickie shook her head. "He's pissed I lied to him. He's pissed he had to find out about it by being attacked by his Gorafrex-possessed best friend. He's pissed that he didn't even see it coming."

"He'll forgive you."

"He already *has*. That's the thing. He forgave me, and he's pissed, and he won't be later, and I should've just told him everything from the beginning."

Laura shifted her weight onto one foot. "That've been worse. You're the one breaking the rules if you openly tell a human about magic and this ship and everything they let themselves forget. It's not your fault if the Gorafrex attacked him. Or even that you did what you had to do to protect him, right?"

"It feels like my fault."

"Well." The oldest Hadstrom sister shrugged. "If you wanna beat yourself up about it, that's up to you. But I think you made the right calls all around."

"Seriously?"

"Yeah. It's what I would've done."

Nickie rolled her eyes. "Yeah, but you don't have to lie to your boyfriend about anything. He's already in the magic club."

"And he's not my boyfriend."

"Might as well be."

Laura pointed at her sister. "Okay, we're not talking about Nathan right now, so don't do that. Deflecting is *my* thing." They laughed. "Besides, Chuck's a really smart guy. You two are good for each other. What's the worst that can happen now that he knows everything? He makes really bad jokes for a while, and Emily'll join in, and we have to just deal with that until it gets old."

"Huh." Nickie blinked and smiled at the image of her boyfriend and her little sister going back and forth with puns about magic. "That's exactly what they'd do."

"I know." Laura swung the giant wrench up and set it on her shoulder. "And when you look at it that way, Nickie, it's really not—"

The ground shuddered beneath their feet, rocking them sideways. Both witches stumbled against the wall, and the wrench slipped from Laura's hand before hitting the floor with a loud *clang*. Seconds later, a roaring echo filled the chamber, drowning Nickie out as she shouted, "What's going on?"

Laura still understood the question and shook her head. "No idea."

A rain of pebbles and loose earth fell from the chamber ceiling. The ground trembled again, and Laura bent to pick up the wrench before she and her sister ran out into the corridor. It was a little quieter, but not by much.

"We're not under an airport this time." Nickie glanced at the dark ceiling.

"I don't think those were planes. I really hope they're

not planes." Laura lifted her hand, and the silver ring on her thumb sputtered out a weak silver light. "No way."

"What?"

"Something's wrong. My ring's acting like it's got a few loose wires." Laura cleared her throat and tried again, focusing on her ring while, all around them, the cavern and corridor trembled with more aftershocks. The small translucent transport bubble bloomed slowly on her ring before being sucked back into it. "Come *on*."

"Lemme try." Nickie cast the spell with her black legacy ring, which glowed with an oddly shimmering brown color. But the transport bubble did what it was supposed to do, growing on her ring before detaching and swelling to its full size.

"There's no way that's me." Laura frowned and stepped into the bubble.

"Nope. That's magic turning sideways." Just before the bubble disappeared and took the Hadstrom witches with it, a section of the stone corridor cracked, and the ceiling caved in with a blast of dirt and cold air.

The minute the bubble burst in their living room, Chuck jumped on the couch with a shout of surprise. "Jeeze! How did you—" He blinked the sleep out of his eyes and sighed. "Oh. Right."

Nickie went to him with a sympathetic smile. "Did you fall asleep?"

"You know that's how I process stuff. And I had a lot of processing to do." He ran a hand through his blond hair and sat back against the couch again. "You guys accomplish your mission?" Both sisters shot him skeptical glances. "Or whatever you call it."

"Not *mission*, babe." Nickie dropped onto the couch beside him and kissed his cheek. "But yeah. It went the way we wanted." She and Laura glanced at each other. "Mostly."

"Okay…that Hadstrom look means you guys are leaving something out." Chuck folded his arms. "Holy crap."

"What?"

"That look!" He pointed at each of them and grinned like a maniac. "I used to think the three of you just had more inside jokes than anyone else on the planet. But that's the look you give each other when you're trying not to talk about magic stuff, huh?"

Laura tried to pull it off like she had no idea what he was talking about, but she and Nickie both knew it wasn't going to work with him. "Wow." She nodded at her sister. "He's good."

"Yeah, well, five years with the Hadstrom girls, you learn a thing or too." Chuck frowned when he realized the missing pieces of what he'd just said. "Except for the fact that you're all witches from a different planet."

"Babe, *we* are not from a different planet. We were born here. Our ancestors stepped off Arenya V thousands of years ago, and that's a completely different thing."

"Okay, okay. So, what aren't you guys saying?"

"Well…"

"Might as well tell him."

Laura folded her arms and sat in the armchair. "Magic's going a little crazy in Austin. At least we hope it's just Austin and not everywhere else."

"What do you mean by crazy?"

"I know all of this is still crazy-sounding to you, babe." Nickie leaned back and offered a thin smile. "But what

MARTHA CARR & MICHAEL ANDERLE

we're talking about is magic not working the way it's supposed to."

"Huh." Chuck scratched his head. "I mean, I don't really know anything, but that doesn't sound very good."

Laura scoffed. "It's not. And we need to figure out how to stop it from getting worse."

"Can you do that?"

Nickie nodded. "Yeah. We're working on it—" Those fast, desperate, urgent drumbeats rose up in her head without warning, sudden and intense. Nickie's temples exploded with pain, and she clenched her eyes shut.

"Uh-oh." Chuck leaned toward her and rubbed her back. "Is it another migraine?"

Nickie couldn't help it. She laughed and could only hear the echo of her own voice over the constant, primal rhythm in her brain. Still, she thought she was laughing like a maniac.

"Woah, okay. What's going on?" Chuck glanced at Laura. "You guys found her migraine meds the other night, right? Shouldn't she still have some?"

Laura wrinkled her nose, then got up and stepped toward the couch. "It's not really that kind of migraine, Chuck. Sorry." She knelt in front of her sister, and he stared at them.

"What kind is it, then?"

"The kind that means the Gorafrex is doing something we're really not gonna like." Laura squeezed her sister's knee and held out her hand. "Nickie, your keys."

"That doesn't make any sense."

"Babe." Nickie grunted and clutched at his arm. She could barely hear herself think enough to form the words she wanted. "I have to go." She pulled her keys from her back pocket.

Laura didn't even wait for her to fumble with them; she grabbed the keys out of Nickie's hand and separated the silver Clubhouse coin from everything else. "Right here." She grabbed Nickie's fingers and guided them toward the thumbprint.

"Wait a minute. Go where?" Chuck smoothed the hair away from Nickie's forehead and frowned. "Hey, talk to me."

"I can't…"

"Chuck." Laura shot him a stern glance that made him freeze. "I'll explain it as soon as we get Nickie somewhere safe, okay?"

"Where's that?"

"The only place the Gorafrex can't get to her. Even in her head."

Nickie's thumb slipped onto the thumbprint in the coin, and she disappeared with a little pop.

"Hey!" Chuck nearly fell over when his girlfriend vanished from beneath his arm. "What did you do?"

"She's fine. I promise." Laura tapped her fingers against her lips and rose from her knees to sit beside him on the couch. "We built this magical room together when we were kids. Called it the Clubhouse, and it just stuck."

"*What?*"

"Come on, Chuck. I'm trying to fill you in, here."

"Yeah, yeah. Clubhouse." He puffed out a sigh and closed his eyes. "I'm trying too."

"I know. This place is kind of in its own dimension. I think." She shrugged. "Doesn't really matter where, just that all three of us can get to it from wherever we are. With these." She pulled her keyring from her pocket to show him. "And no one else can get in."

"What about me?" Chuck blinked, already knowing the answer but asking anyway.

"No one else, Chuck. Sorry."

"Yeah…" He cleared his throat and stared at her keys. "What just happened?"

Laura bit her lip and frowned at him. "Nickie can hear the Gorafrex's magic in her head. Seeing as the last time she heard it was when…well, when it found Dave, this time means the thing's either trying to lure another witch or wizard, or…"

"Or what?" She shook her head, and Chuck slapped his thighs. "Laura. Or what?"

"Or it's using it's magic to activate another energy core with that witch or wizard's lifeforce magic."

"Okay, pretend I'm still learning what all that means."

"It means there's another witch or wizard out there we *couldn't* save. And it means things are about to get a lot weirder, magic-wise." Nickie's boyfriend rubbed his mouth and stared at her with wide eyes. "Yeah, I hope I'm wrong too."

CHAPTER TWENTY-TWO

"If I didn't already know what you do for a living, I would've pegged you as someone who seriously doesn't enjoy fine dining." John tossed his wrapper from their cheaper and far more successful dinner into the trashcan beside the food truck.

Emily spread her arms and shrugged. "I'm obviously not feeling like myself." *And, apparently, I can't keep my magic under control. First, I pour my emotions into food that other people eat and feel everything I do, and now I've got magical telekinesis issues when I'm nervous. Why am I nervous?*

John eyed her and tilted his head. "You're trying to work something out right now."

"That obvious, huh?"

He pointed at her temple and leaned forward. "I can see the gears turning." With a sympathetic smile, he added, "Anything I can do to help?"

Just tell us exactly how to get the Gorafrex out of human hosts so we can lock it up where it belongs and get back to normal life. "I don't think so, honestly. But thanks." She sucked down the rest of her blueberry lemonade in the paper cup and tossed it in the trash. "It means a lot that you wanna help, though."

"That's what happens when you like somebody, right?" He stepped toward her and hooked his finger under her chin. "'Cause I really like you, Em."

The only thing Emily could do was smile until she was kissing him back. When he pulled away, she wrinkled her nose a little. "Yeah, you're not too bad, either."

John laughed and grabbed her hand. "Okay, so I *was* planning on taking you to this karaoke bar downtown…"

She laughed. "I never pegged you as a karaoke guy."

"Well, I'm not Frank Sinatra or anything, but there's nothing like entertainment via watching people sing their hearts out after a few too many drinks. Sometimes someone shows up with actual talent, and then it feels like waiting through all the screeching was worth it."

They walked away from the food truck, the sun barely hanging on above the western horizon. "Let me just say that Nickie's the only one who's got any musical talent whatsoever. You'll be sorely disappointed by me."

"I bet you're better than you think."

"Not when our lazy bulldog who doesn't get up for anything but food and a soft bed leaves the room every time I sing."

John gave her a joking wince. "That bad, huh?"

"Probably worse."

He chuckled. "All right. I made the right call then. No karaoke. How 'bout a walk in the park?"

Emily raised an eyebrow. "Goin' old-fashioned, huh?"

"You've never gone on a date and just walked around outside?"

She shrugged. "The last guy I was with was into gourmet food and video games. So no. Not really."

"We're gonna change that."

They'd stopped for street food next to the Emma Long Metropolitan Park on the north side of town, so walking to their new destination to just keep walking didn't take long. The park was lit with a few streetlamps beside the road and the parking lot, giving plenty of light before the rest of daylight faded after sunset. John stopped at the edge of the first path and gestured to the grass and dogwood trees and well-kept open space in front of them. "Care for a stroll, madam?" He offered her his elbow and waited.

Emily pulled her best snobby-aristocrat face and batted her eyelashes. "Such a gentleman." She hooked her arm through his, and they fought the urge to crack up.

The park was fairly empty on a Tuesday night, with just a few people finishing up their own outdoor adventures. A man in his late sixties jogged past and nodded. "Man, I hope I can still move like that at seventy."

Emily glanced back at the man and smiled. "Better start now, then, right? I bet the guy's been running most of his life."

John frowned. "I'm not actually that into running."

"Oh, so this is the part where we share our totally unattainable goals and laugh about how we'll never actually get there?"

"Ha." He gave her hand on his arm a quick little pat. "You really get me, Em." The way she laughed at that part made him grin, and he took in a deep breath of the evening air that had slipped down beneath the steamy, warm-blanket temperatures. "My favorite park is actually Ladybird."

Emily blinked at him. "I'm just gonna give you the benefit of the doubt and say you had no idea where I lived until I texted you my address this morning."

That confused him a few seconds until he understood and snorted. "That *is* pretty close to you, isn't it? I promise I haven't been stalking you."

"Yeah, no big deal. We just work at the same restaurant and your favorite park happens to be super close to my house." Emily grinned and liked that John didn't take her sarcasm too seriously. *So many people do.*

"This one's pretty nice. Not much traffic on the paths." He frowned and looked at the darkening sky. "It's a little quiet, though. You notice that?"

"Oh, yeah." Emily bit her lip and followed his gaze. "I think there are usually more birds." *Like the grackles that fell outta the sky. That's definitely what's missing.*

"Yeah, maybe."

Ten minutes later, they stopped at one of the benches beside the path as John finished his childhood story. "I think we had fried turkey every day for at last three weeks after that."

Emily shook her head. "Was this before cell phones?"

"Nope." He laughed. "My parents just refuse to use theirs. They still have a landline."

When he sat on the bench, Emily lowered beside him and didn't miss that his arm went over her shoulders across the back of the bench. She scooted closer and leaned into him. "I think I've taken the lead on every Thanksgiving dinner since I was a freshman in high school."

"Wow."

"Yeah, that's how much I love what I do. One of my aunts wasn't happy about it. But she can't cook, and everyone knew it, so nobody said anything. She turned to what she calls 'crafting' instead."

"Crafting what?"

"Literally anything." Emily widened her eyes and stared at him. "Like elf slippers and the ugliest holiday sweaters you've ever seen. And cat pillows."

John snorted. "Everyone's got their gifts, I guess."

"Or not."

They were silent for a bit, listening to a few birds twittering in the trees around them. The lampposts scattered around the park lay bright pools of light over the grass. "How's your leg?"

"What?"

John nodded at her knee, which was no longer bouncing . "Your muscle cramps."

"Oh. Those. Yeah, it's feeling a lot better."

"Good." He grinned and leaned toward her. "I had a feeling a walk might help with some of that."

Oh, man. That sounds like he knows I was lying. Emily forced a smile. "Well, good thinking on your part." She turned toward him and glanced at his lips. *Talk about old-fashioned date night, making out on a park bench.* "Does that mean you're taking back that free massage offer?"

He leaned closer, slipped his hand below her ear toward the back of her neck, and whispered, "Absolutely not."

Emily could have sat there with John on that park bench all night just kissing him, but that bit of wishful thinking was shattered by the loud, cracking *boom* that came from all around them. She and John leapt away from each other, and they gazed around with wide eyes. "What was that?"

"I have no idea." Emily slid her hand down his chest, gave him a reassuring pat, and rose from the bench. "But I don't think—"

The ground rocked beneath her feet, sending her off balance and into John's lap.

He caught her, but it wasn't one of those cute moments between a new couple when tripping and being clumsy was endearing. John looked terrified. "Is this an earthquake?"

"I mean, Texas *has* been getting a lot more of those late-ly." *And I seriously wonder how many of them have been from the energy cores, destroyed or activated.* "I'm not sure that's it, though."

"Okay. We should get back to my car."

"Wouldn't this be the safest place during an earthquake? Out in the open with nothing huge to fall on us?" She glanced behind him and saw a wave of shimmering blue light seeping up from the path they'd taken to the bench. *Or we're in the most dangerous place to be caught up in a bunch of magic gone wrong.* "I'm gonna go check it out."

When she stood from his lap, John grabbed her wrist. "Hey, I'm not sure that's such a good idea." He still hadn't seen the magical light rising behind him like smoke, and Emily didn't want him to.

"I'll be fine. It's better to know what's going on, right?"

"What can you even check out about an earthquake?"

Emily smiled and gently pulled away. When she turned around to head somewhere so she could tune into the wayward magic out here without being obvious about it, she froze.

A vaguely human-shaped ten-foot tall form was plodding toward the park. With every step, the ground shook—not as much as it had with that first explosive boom but enough for Emily to feel in her feet. A few birds flew from their nests just before the giant creature's shoulder brushed against the tree branches.

Emily retreated. "At least we know it's not an earthquake. Mostly."

"What *is* that thing?" The only part of John's body that hadn't frozen was his mouth, which seemed to keep going despite how much he knew he should be running away. "It's huge. How did it get that big? I'm not...this isn't... Emily, are you seeing this?"

"If you are," she muttered without turning to look at him, "then, yeah, we're seeing it together."

"Oh, God." John sucked in a deep breath.

CHAPTER TWENTY-THREE

The massive creature stepped under a lamppost, almost knocking the light off with the top of its head. It reeled, grunted, and stooped to squint up at the bottom of the light. "It's like they've taken everything we've done and gone backward with it," the thing muttered. "Stupidest thing I ever saw. And now they're *destroying* what's left of it." A massive hand smacked against the lamppost and bent it at a small angle.

"It can talk," John said.

"That's what it looks like." Emily stared at the creature beneath the lamppost, and now that it was in more light, the young witch realized 'it' was actually a 'she'—a massive woman in an olive-green jumpsuit with patches of brown, gray, and tan, her gray hair piled on top of her head as if she'd knotted it there on purpose. Huge, dark eyes blinked from behind what looked like magnification goggles as the woman scowled and scanned the dark sky and the first of the stars out for the night.

"That's an Engineer," Emily muttered.

"A what?"

She turned to glance at John and shook her head. "Nothing, I just…" *Gotta make it sound like you have no idea what's going on, Em.* "Does that look like a woman to you?"

"Emily, I don't think any woman grows that big."

The massive woman beneath the lamppost stomped her foot and roared at the open sky. "Where is everyone? I've been trying to send messages for days! That's immensely difficult to accomplish when *none of the messengers answer my summons.*"

"Uh-oh…"

John grabbed her hand. "Hey, we need to go."

"It's just a giant angry woman yelling in the middle of the park, John. No big deal."

"Seriously big deal. It's a 'bigger than any person should ever be' kinda deal. Come on."

The Engineer stomped away from the lamppost, shaking the ground with her massive boots that could have been boulders. Emily and John almost toppled backward onto the bench. The giant woman reached into one of the many pockets of her jumpsuit and pulled out a screwdriver every bit as huge and heavy-looking as Laura's Velikan socket wrench. The woman shook her tool at the sky and the trees. "I don't play games, I'll have you know. If the messengers don't come to me, I'll come to them. *Where are the Tree Folk?* Why am I being ignored?" She stumbled sideways a little, her magnified eyes behind the goggles clenching shut, then growled in frustration. "I can *feel* the ship malfunctioning, you cowardly imbeciles. *What happened?*"

Emily swallowed. *That would totally be our fault.*

The Engineer thrust her screwdriver toward the closest tree, and a blue light shot from the tip to encompass the entire plant—roots, trunk, branches, and leaves—in a swirling blue dome. "Someone needs to tell me why this ship is in so much pain." The tree in her magical embrace shuddered despite the lack of a breeze strong enough to blow it like that. Bright dots of light in every color pulsed up the tree trunk, then another wave of rustling leaves and swaying branches spread outward from the glowing tree. The others around it moved in unison, sending a ripple effect of voiceless conversation through the park.

Oh, great. Now she's getting her information from the trees. Emily wanted to go to the Velikan woman, but a higher-than-normal voice came from behind her.

"What—" John's voice cracked under the one word, and he cleared his throat. "I'm not seeing this."

"Crap." Emily turned toward him, her mouth opening and closing as she thought of something to say, anything to explain away her new and very human boyfriend was seeing magic right out in the open. "This isn't what it looks like." *Oh, good job, Em.*

"I don't even know what it looks like!" John couldn't pull his stare away from the giant woman throwing blue light out of a giant screwdriver. "This is insane!"

From behind the Engineer, came the rise and fall of police sirens. As soon as they echoed into the park, they cut off.

Three transport bubbles appeared between the Velikan Engineer and where Emily and John gaped at her, and three Huldu gnomes went running across the grass the moment the bubbles popped. Two of them headed for the Engineer, and the third made a beeline for Emily and John.

"Okay." The gnome stopped, huffing a little to catch his breath, and scowled at Emily. "Since you're more inclined to listen and not freak out about every little thing, is there anyone else in the park?"

Emily glanced around and shook her head. "I don't think so. Just us."

The gnome nodded, then glanced from her to John and back again. "A witch and a human, huh?" He shook his head. "People are always trying to make things difficult."

"Wait a minute, what?" John gaped at the Huldu mechanic. "Forget giant women and tiny dudes—"

"Hey, watch it, pal." The gnome folded his arms.

"Did you just say witch?"

Rolling his eyes, the gnome scoffed and looked at Emily. "Not a very smart human, though, is he?"

She tried not to wrinkle her nose at the scent of damp earth and decaying leaves coming off the Huldu. Emily nodded toward the Engineer, who howled in outrage at the two gnomes failing to calm her. "What's going on?"

"Burst right up out of the ground." The gnome spread his arms, his short-cut goatee twitching with his lips in agitation. "Ripped off the back side of the museum downtown, so that's gonna be an expensive fix. Time-wise, of course. Had a whole bunch of people running around and screaming their heads off at the sight of *a giant* stomping across the city. We've been following her the whole way trying to clean up her mess."

"I'm guessing that's been working out." Emily gave the gnome a sympathetic smile.

"Given the fact we're not supposed to be *up* here in the first place, sure. It's perfect. Nobody'll remember a thing."

With another roar, the Engineer swiped her huge arm toward one of the gnomes beside her to bat him away. The Huldu conjured a shield with good shock-absorbers just in time and skidded backward across the grass.

"She will, though, won't she?"

The Huldu shrugged. "Dunno. Velikan remember everything, up until they live so long that their brain eats itself." He scrunched up his face at John, who'd lowered himself onto the park bench.

"I think I might be able to talk her down," said Emily.

"Ha!" The gnome belched, jumped in surprise, and thumped himself on the chest. "Sorry, witch. This might be a little beyond your wand-waving skills."

"I don't need a wand." Emily showed him the ring on her thumb, and the gnome's eyes widened. "And my sister had a nice chat with that Engineer just a week ago."

"Huh." With a shrug, the gnome cocked his head. "Knock yourself out, kid."

"John." Emily turned toward him and reached for his hand. "I know this is hard to—"

A bright-pink bubble burst from the gnome's hand, floated in front of John's face, then flashed a brilliant light right in his eyes. Emily's date let out a little groan and slumped back on the bench, unconscious.

"Hey!" Emily glared at the gnome. "I was working on it."

"Not fast enough, you weren't." The gnome frowned at her as he stepped toward his fellows trying to reason with the infuriated Engineer. "Gotta close *all* the loopholes. I'm sure you understand." He waved a dismissive hand at John. "He'll wake up a little dizzy and wondering why he can't remember the past half hour. You're welcome."

"Oh, boy." She bent over John's head propped against the back of the bench and gently brushed her hand across his forehead. "I'm so sorry. But I think it's actually better this way. I'm not supposed to tell you what's—"

A loud whistle interrupted her, and the gnome trotted backward with his hand flung out toward the raging Engineer. "Put your money where your mouth is, kid. You coming or what?"

"Right." With a last glance at her passed-out date, Emily gritted her teeth and headed across the park behind the rude Huldu and toward the last living Velikan Engineer.

The two other gnomes were having no luck calming her. One sent a bright white bubble at her hand, which knocked the massive screwdriver out of her grasp. The blue light around the closest tree sputtered and went out, and all the other trees became still.

"Have you lost your minds?" the Engineer roared, glaring at the Huldu with comically magnified eyes. "The trees are the only ones willing to talk to me. Everyone else on the surface has clammed up like a—" Her gaze fell on Emily, and those huge eyes blinked.

"Friend of yours?" the gnome asked in a flat, unamused voice.

"What?" The Engineer glared at him. "I've never seen this witch before."

"You've met my sister." Emily stuck her finger in the air, like it was a good idea to show how well she could make her point, then lowered it again. "Laura Hadstrom?"

"Hadstrom?" The woman straightened with a grunt and sniffed the air. "That name is so…"

"You're Rutilda, right?"

For a few seconds, the park was silent as the last Engineer and three Huldu mechanics blinked at the young witch. The Velikan woman narrowed her eyes. "How do you know my name?"

"My sister told me." *Yeah, she's totally losing her mind.* "Laura Hadstrom. She came to visit you about a week ago to talk about the—" Emily glanced at the gnomes and licked her lips. "The problem with a prison break and a… small vessel needing some mechanical work." *Definitely not a good idea to just say it all out in the open. Assuming none of the Huldu know about the mess we're trying to clean up.*

The gnome who'd wiped John's memory snorted. "Kid, if anything on this ship needed mechanical work, you think we wouldn't already know about it?" The other two sniggered. "This one designed it, but we keep things running—"

"*Nothing* is running at optimal performance," Rutilda hissed. "And who failed to keep this ship sailing toward its final destination in the first place?"

The Huldu stared at her. "Okay, fine. We *try* to keep things running. We do our best." He thrust a fat finger toward the Engineer and leaned forward. "Don't forget that none of us were actually *here* when that happened, okay? You can blame our great-great-grandfathers, if you have to blame someone."

"*I* was here." Rutilda's voice lowered into a snarl, and she bent her aged back to rest her hands against her knees and stick her giant nose into the gnome's face. "This ship was designed to perfection, Huldu. Someone failed in performing their sworn duties."

The gnome with the goatee swallowed and glanced at his fellows. "Point taken." He shot Emily a sideways glance. "She's all yours, kid. Try not to get stomped on." With that, the Huldu snapped his fingers, and all three popped out of the park.

Emily rolled her eyes and muttered, "Yeah, nice to meet you too." Then she felt Rutilda turning her magnified stare onto the young witch. "You too, of course." *And if I can't get this Engineer to calm down, I'm in a lot of trouble.*

CHAPTER TWENTY-FOUR

E mily swallowed as the Velikan Engineer glowered down at her. "Please tell me you remember my sister."

Rutilda narrowed her magnified eyes, then exploded into a long, wheezing cackle. She pushed up off her knees, grunting through laughter as she straightened. Emily heard the ancient woman's spine creaking. The engineer slapped a knee and shook her head. "Of *course* I remember your sister."

"Oh. I thought maybe you'd—"

"That I was losing my mind? That I've gone far too senile to be *allowed* aboveground?"

"Uh...maybe?"

Rutilda waved a dismissive hand and tilted her head. "Had to get rid of the Huldu, didn't I? They're well-intentioned, of course. I know this. And the fewer people who know about your sister's dangerous little secret, the better."

"I agree with you on that one." Emily scratched her head and couldn't help a little chuckle when she realized how well the Engineer had lied to the Mechanics. "So, you know about my sister—"

"And her secrets, yes. Laura Hadstrom, archaeologist, oldest of three, and the witch responsible for freeing the Gorafrex from its prison."

"Yeah, that part was an accident."

"So she claimed." The woman raised an eyebrow and smacked her wrinkled lips. "It would seem she told her sisters all about the little chat we had."

"Well, we sort of tell each other everything. At least the important stuff." Emily gave the woman an unsure smile and shrugged. "I'm pretty sure I can answer some of your questions."

"What do you know of my questions, little Emily Hadstrom?"

"Um…" The young witch glanced around at the park and the trees, all of them still once more. "Not like I was trying to hear you or anything. I'm kind of on a—" Emily glanced over her shoulder at John on the bench and shook her head. "Well, I *was* on a date. But you were kinda screaming your questions out one right after the other, so…"

The Engineer wheezed with heavy laughter and shook a giant finger at the witch. "I like you, Emily Hadstrom. Your sister tried very hard to be polite with me. Too hard, one might say."

"Yeah, she tends to do that."

"Ha! And you eliminate any form of pretense whatsoever. I enjoy this very much, Emily Hadstrom." The Engineer chuckled and folded her arms. A few bits of dust and rock and what looked like a massive slug fell from the folds of the woman's jumpsuit. "Now, if you can answer my questions, I suggest you do so quickly. I haven't been aboveground in far too long, and I must say it's too bright for my liking."

"It's…" Emily glanced at the black sky and the few stars she could see despite the streetlamps. "Really?"

Rutilda grunted in response.

"Okay, I'll try to be fast. You told my sister the symbol we found in that house, the symbol drawn in another witch's blood, was a blueprint of another smaller ship built inside this one. With the Gorafrex's prison at the middle."

"Your sister was adamant about calling it an *escape pod*." Rutilda's eyes narrowed.

"Yeah, I heard about that. I also heard you really don't like that name, so I figured I wouldn't use it."

The Engineer hummed in approval and smiled. "Go on."

"We've been destroying the energy cores. That wrench is pretty awesome, by the way."

"Good. How many?"

Emily looked up and counted in her head. "Five, so far."

"Hmm. Not quite enough."

"Well, we're gonna get another one tomorrow. Then the ship can't be powered up at all, right?"

"It needs only half to operate successfully, not fully, yes. And I assume you're keeping the Gorafrex from activating any of the others until you can destroy them all?"

"Not exactly…"

Rutilda sucked in a quick breath through her teeth, her eyes growing wide. "And how many has the creature awakened with its blood magic?"

"One." Emily nodded curtly. "And a half."

"Ancestors save us." The Engineer whirled and faced the trees. "The trees know many things. The pressures beneath the surface. The taste of magic in the air. The changes." She reached out to gently stroke the closest branch and glanced down at Emily. "Now it makes sense. The Tree Folk are terrified. Magic turned on its head, rearranged into all the wrong forms. The ship's magic only fuels that damage."

"We've noticed." Emily scrunched up her nose and hoped the woman wouldn't lose it again. *But she deserves to hear everything, right? I mean, she did burst up out of a cavern under the museum. That's worth something.* "And your messages. They haven't been delivered, because the magic that's going crazy everywhere got to the grackles first."

Rutilda scowled. "What happened to the messengers, Emily Hadstrom?"

"They kind of...fell out of the sky. Onto our house. A lot are in our side yard, actually."

With a heavy sigh, the last Engineer shook her head. A shiver of dust sprayed from her gray hair. "You must end this. You and your sisters, yes? The three of you are the only ones who can."

"We know." Emily stepped forward, realizing this might be the moment they got the rest of the answers they needed. "Laura had this idea to recreate the binding rune that was on the prison. We can capture it that way."

"That is...surprisingly creative." Rutilda stroked her chin. "And you will return it to the prison that way?"

"I guess we have to figure out one more step." Emily let out a frustrated sigh. "It's not like we can drop an iron weapon through a rock in the Greenbelt."

"Hmm." With a smirk, the Engineer glanced up at the sky. "Perhaps the rune should include physical transference of some form."

"Like a transportation bubble?"

Rutilda barked another wheezing laugh. "That is Peabrain magic, yes. And yet the humans have never had the misfortune of capturing a Gorafrex. No, Emily Hadstrom, I am referring to a transference that is instantaneous. From one place to another in the blink of an eye."

"Okay. I'll let Laura figure that one out."

"As you wish."

"Hey, you wouldn't happen to know how to get the Gorafrex *out* of a host so we can actually *use* the rune, do you?"

"Ah." Rutilda rubbed her huge hands together and bent to retrieve her screwdriver from the path. "Have you ever seen a *caporchian* feed on its mate?"

"Nope."

"Perhaps a surface-dweller analogy would be more suitable." The Engineer slipped her massive tool into one of her jumpsuit's pockets and nodded. "Salt on a slug."

"Um…what?"

"It's a simple matter of alchemy, Emily Hadstrom. The salt draws all the moisture out of the slug through its flesh and dries its mucous secretions. It's quite messy, yes? And it kills the slug. But the process, I imagine, is very much like that you must use with the Gorafrex."

Emily frowned and crossed her arms. "Yeah, but a human host isn't a slug. And we don't want to kill whoever it is once we get that thing out of their body."

"I understand. You will do what you must." Rutilda

coughed a few times before spitting onto the grass beside them. A puff of dust escaped her mouth, followed by something that looked very much like a dust-covered moth, especially when it fluttered away into the trees. "I imagine you might find a way to tailor the alchemical reaction to a very specific purpose with some very specific magic."

"I know you spend a lot of time by yourself," Emily said, "but I still didn't understand anything you just said."

"Indeed." When the Velikan woman grinned, her wrinkled lips pulled back to reveal huge, yellow-stained teeth. "What, Emily Hadstrom, combines alchemy and magic to produce a physical tool one might use for its intended purpose? A tool anyone might use, whether or not that being knows its purpose or that magic exists in the first place?"

Emily glanced around the empty park, silent but for the buzzing insects in the warm night air and the loud, slow breathing of the giant woman in front of her. *Slugs...* The only connection she made to that was the state of their greenhouse and all the plants that had somehow grown out of proportion with varying degrees of dangerous new properties. "Oh. You mean alchemy like chemistry, don't you?"

"If that's what everyone's calling it these days."

"Chemistry *and* magic." The young witch grinned. "You could've just told me, 'There's a potion for that,' Rutilda. That would've saved us a few minutes."

"Ha! At least you understand."

"Yeah, okay. A potion to suck the Gorafrex right out of the host."

Rutilda nodded. "Salt on a slug."

Emily snorted. "When I find a different analogy that doesn't end up *killing* the human, I'm gonna find you and tell you to use that one instead."

The Velikan Engineer threw her head back and roared with laughter. The few trees around her swayed in a rustle of branches, and the woman hunched over. "Oh, yes. I forget I cannot be as loud up here as I wish." Her hand fluttered toward the rest of the park around them. "Other living things being what they are."

"I hear ya. People tell me to cut it out all the time."

"I like you very much, Emily Hadstrom." Rutilda tried as best she could to hold back another cackle.

Emily studied the woman's mussed hair and dusty jumpsuit and huge, magnified eyes. "I like you too."

Rutilda chuckled and shook her head. "May you and your sisters finish what you started as soon as possible so I can get back to the end of my life. I was growing fond of how it was all turning out."

"Oh. Okay." Emily blinked as the Engineer turned and headed south toward downtown. "Just one more question…"

"Yes?"

"How do we keep magic from getting worse? Is that even possible?"

"I do not know, Emily Hadstrom. I will say the only way to reverse the effects is to destroy the energy cores the creature has already awakened, but if that image your sister showed me is correct, it was done with blood magic. Meaning you will not destroy those activated cores until the Gorafrex is in its iron prison and weakened enough it must release its hold on that magic. I do not recommend destroying activated cores before such time."

"Right. Thank you." Emily lifted her hand for a little wave, and the Engineer chuckled before shuffling off.

"Do your worst with it, then. You are far from the end." Without turning around to say goodbye, the giant woman who'd designed and built this ship centuries ago with her brethren disappeared through the trees lining the park.

Emily watched until all signs of the Engineer's path had faded. "I wonder how she's gonna get back under the museum."

A groan sounded from behind her, and she spun to see John sitting up, rubbing his neck. *I can't believe I forgot about him.* The young witch jogged toward him and sat beside her date. "Are you okay?"

"I...don't know." John blinked, opened his eyes wide, and closed them tightly again. "My head's killing me."

"Yeah, you said you might be coming down with something."

"I did?"

"Yep. See? You've got the brain fog too. Come on." She grabbed his wrist and pulled him slowly to his feet. "I have no problem driving back to my house, but you'll have to take it from there if you wanna get back to your place tonight. I'm sure you'll be fine once you walk it off." *Isn't that what he told me about my 'muscle cramps'?*

"Em, I'm so sorry. I don't even...I mean, I had tonight all planned out...it didn't include this." John twirled his finger at the park and rubbed his forehead.

"John, do not worry about it at all. We'll have plenty of other dates."

He glanced up at her, trying to smile through his severe dizziness. "Promise?"

"Totally. Trust me, this isn't even close to the worst date I've ever had." That made him laugh, and Emily helped him put his arm around her shoulder so she could support him more. They walked down the path toward the parking lot, and she took a deep breath. *The worst date would be the one he doesn't remember.*

CHAPTER TWENTY-FIVE

E mily grabbed the open driver-side door as John slipped behind the wheel. "You sure you're good to drive?"

"Yeah. It's not like I had a lot to drink." He blinked at the steering wheel and shot her a worried glance. "We didn't drink a lot tonight, did we?"

"No. I think we had one glass of wine each..."

"Okay. Cool. Man, I can't believe my brain just stopped working."

She leaned down toward him and put a hand on his shoulder. "Seriously, don't worry about it. Go home. Get some rest. You'll feel better in the morning."

"I hope so." She started to turn away from his car, but he grabbed her hand. "Hey. Thanks."

"For what?"

"For not being super upset tonight didn't go the way either of us planned." John shrugged. "For not being upset at all, actually."

Emily squeezed his hand and kissed the corner of his mouth. "Like I said, this definitely isn't the worst date. And we'll have more. We don't have to bring this one up again, okay?"

"Deal. You working tomorrow?"

"Yep."

"I'll see you then."

With a nod, she stepped away from the open door and grabbed it again. "Perfect. Good night."

"'Night, Em."

She closed his car door, and he watched her step up onto the sidewalk before he turned around and drove down Pressler Street the way they'd come. Emily went up the concrete steps toward the front of her house and got all the way to the door before she realized she'd seen an extra car parked on the curb. "Mine, Laura's, Nickie's. Yeah, that's Chuck's car. So, who drives the Jeep?" Squinting at the blue Jeep parked behind Chuck's sedan, she twisted the doorknob and stepped inside.

The voices in the living room stopped, and she shut the door behind her before seeing Laura, Chuck, and Nathan sitting there. "Huh." *Definitely wasn't expecting Nathan to be here when I got home from a magically-interrupted date.* "Hey, guys."

"Did you have a good time?" Laura didn't sound remotely interested in her answer.

"Uh...I'll answer that later." Emily walked through the foyer and jerked her thumb over her shoulder. "Nathan, is that your Jeep out front?"

"Yep. I just got here."

"Cool Jeep." The youngest Hadstrom sister frowned and glanced behind her into the dining room. "Where's Nickie?"

"Clubhouse," Laura said.

Emily glanced at Chuck, then shot her sister the 'not in front of a human' look they'd all learned to use since the guy had started dating their sister. "Okay…"

Chuck spread his arms. "The drums again, apparently."

An exaggerated laugh burst out of Emily's mouth, and she pointed at him. "Good one, Chuck. I have no idea what you're talking about, but it's funny." *How the heck does he know about the drums?*

"Em?"

"Yeah."

Laura tapped a fist against Chuck's arm where they sat together on the couch. "He knows."

Emily's smile fell off her face. "Knows what, Laura?" She glanced at Nathan, who smiled a little in amusement as he watched the revelation unfold.

"Everything."

"Um…" Emily glanced at each of them in turn one more time, and her lips formed the shapes of words she didn't think she wanted to use. She settled on, "Somebody please tell me what's going on."

"Witches. Magic. Aliens trying to kill witches and take their magic." Chuck ran a hand through his hair. "When she says everything, Em, she means everything. I sound like a crazy person saying this out loud, but I believe all of it. That thing tried to kill me *and* Nickie today. Oh, yeah. And it's inside Dave now."

Laughter bubbled up Emily's throat despite how inappropriate she knew it was. "What are you *talking* about?"

"Em, it's not a joke." Laura shook her head.

"Okay, but...okay." Slowly, the youngest Hadstrom sister took a few more steps into the living room. "I'm out of ideas, so please."

"Chuck and Nickie went to go sign her record deal." Laura glanced at her sister's boyfriend, who nodded before resting his forearms on his thighs and hanging his head. "Sounds like the Gorafrex already had his new host, which just so happened to be the owner of Blue—"

"Yeah, Laura, I know who Dave is. I had no idea Nickie was signing a record deal today. That's awesome." When Emily got only blank stares all around, she realized her mistake. "Which I'm guessing didn't actually happen."

"That thing took over Dave's body," Chuck added, staring at the area rug. "Started blasting magic all over the place at Nickie and me." He looked at Emily and raised his thumb and pointer finger to demonstrate. "Little tiny round thing, Em. This big. Touched me on the shoulder and threw me into a bookshelf."

"Ouch."

"Ha. Yeah, ouch. And your sister..." The man shook his head and grabbed it with both hands. "She did whatever magicky thing I guess witches do. Just a bunch of light that ate up the little red things—*jeeze*. I sound insane."

"Well, this whole thing is kind of insane, Chuck. So is the fact that you know about magic now—"

"Em..." Laura shook her head.

The youngest witch sighed and came to sit on the other side of Nickie's boyfriend. "*You* don't sound insane. You aren't insane, okay?" She pushed her fist against his arm and looked reassuring. "This stuff is real."

"No kidding."

"And we're working on making it all right again." Emily caught her sister's gaze, and Laura gave her a nod of approval. "So...Nathan."

"Emily." The part-Kashgar professor leaned back in one of the armchairs, one ankle crossed over his knee, and picked at his lower lip.

"Why are *you* here?"

"Emily, don't be rude."

"What? It's a fair question."

"No, it's okay." Nathan rubbed his hands together and gathered his thoughts. "Laura asked me to come by so we could examine that rune more. I didn't know Chuck was gonna be here with a whole new outlook on life."

Chuck snorted. "And I had no idea I was gonna be sitting down with a witch and a Casper."

"Kashgar," Nathan corrected, then held up his own thumb and index finger just like Chuck had. "Just a little, though."

"I don't even know what that means."

"Okay, you two." Laura flashed a tight smile at everyone in the living room, trying to bring the focus back to what they needed to do. "Chuck, you can stay here if you want. Feel free to throw in any ideas you might have, whatever they are. Anything could help. Em, there are a few things I should fill you in on first."

"Yeah, that goes both ways, I think." Emily patted Chuck's back before she stood and went to the armchair beside Nathan's, just because things were starting to feel a little crowded. "You wanna go first?"

"Sure."

Nathan folded his arms and sat back to watch the information overload and two witchy sisters come up with a plan.

CHAPTER TWENTY-SIX

"We totally beat the Gorafrex at the energy-core race." Emily grinned. "That's a *good* thing."

"Yeah, Em. It can't launch the escape pod into space, but now we have to keep it from activating the other five cores."

"Because of magic going cuckoo. Right. You know, if I'd known you and Nickie went off by yourselves to break another energy core, I would've been able to give Rutilda the *right* numbers."

Laura shrugged. "Well, you said you weren't gonna let this little Gorafrex issue ruin your night with John, so we were trying to respect that."

"Ruined it anyway, though. I don't know if it's better or worse that he can't remember anything." Emily pointed at Chuck and frowned. "How come *he* didn't get bubble-flashed by a Huldu?"

"Probably because the Huldu don't have any idea what the three of you are dealing with right now," Nathan said.

"Which is honestly pretty impressive. They keep an eye on everything."

"I betcha it has something to do with the fact that the messengers are camping out in our yard instead of telling the whole world about our escaped convict trying to blow up Austin with misfired magic."

"Wow." Nathan chuckled and dipped his head at Emily. "You sure do have a way with descriptions, don't you?"

Emily grinned. "Thank you, Nathan."

"Okay, so we need to figure out the next steps." Laura tapped her finger against her lips.

"I told Rutilda I'd leave this one up to you," Emily said. "Something about physical transference and doing it instantly. From one place to another like that." She snapped her fingers. "Better than a transport bubble, which I don't really understand—"

"Oh!" Laura's dark eyes lit up when the pieces all came together. "She was talking about transference with the rune, right?"

"Uh, I think so."

"That makes so much sense." Laura stood abruptly from the couch, making the cushions bounce a little. Chuck kept staring at the rug and didn't react. "I mean, obviously it'll have to be on a much larger scale and a lot stronger, but that really might work."

"Laura?" Emily watched her sister move back and forth across the living room. "Maybe stop pacing for a minute and explain that a little bit. None of us can read minds."

Chuck looked at her. "You can't?" When Emily shook her head, he just hung his head and picked up where he left off staring at the rug.

"The Clubhouse, Em."

"Is…where Nickie's hanging out right now…"

"No, physical transference. That's instant too. We only knew enough about it when we were kids to build the Clubhouse and the keyring charms, but we can do a *lot* more than that, now."

Emily squinted at her sister until the answer struck her. "Make the new rune pop the Gorafrex right back *into* the prison."

"Exactly."

"Once we get it out of Dave."

Chuck groaned, and Laura's smile faded. "Well, yeah. That's also correct. Which you're gonna get started on too, right, Em?"

"Oh, yeah. I've never made a potion in my life, but yeah. I'll get started on the most important potion I'll probably ever make, like, ever." She cleared her throat.

"I have faith in you."

"Thanks…"

Laura stopped pacing, glanced at her wristwatch, and turned to Nathan. "It's ten-thirty. We can still take a shot at dissecting that first rune, if you wanna stick around for a little longer."

"I'm here, and I'm ready to help." Nathan smiled and shot her a thumbs-up. Emily snorted.

"I'm not gonna be able to sleep…" Chuck shook his head. "Are you guys sure Nickie's okay?"

"She's safe from the drumming, at least." Emily shrugged. "Guess we won't know when it goes away until she comes back and—"

With a little pop of air, Nickie reappeared on the couch

next to Chuck, who nearly leapt over the armrest. She laughed, reached out to rub his arm, and gave him a sympathetic smile. "You're still here."

Her boyfriend blinked a few times and sank back down into the couch. "*Yeah*, I'm still here. You think I was just gonna go home and wait to hear from anybody who thought about telling me how you're doing?"

Nickie slipped her arm through his and leaned against him. "I didn't think that for a second. Sorry to make you wait so long."

"It was only an hour," Laura said. "Did the drums *just* stop?"

Nickie rolled her eyes. "No. This whole magic-going-off-the-rails thing is getting old really fast. I've been trying to get out of the Clubhouse for the last fifteen minutes."

"Uh-oh."

"Yeah, Em." Nickie nodded at her sister and smoothed her hair away from her face. "That's what I thought."

"Wait, what's uh-oh?" Chuck looked at his girlfriend with wide blue eyes. "You're okay, right?"

"I'm okay, babe. Don't worry."

"That just means we have to come up with a Plan B in case the keychains act up again."

"Well, we have the transport bubbles, right?" Nickie nodded. "Those worked before as a last resort. I mean, they're fast enough to avoid magical explosions."

"Magical *what*?" Chuck gulped.

"That we totally caused," Emily added.

"That doesn't make me feel any better."

Laura stepped beside the couch and folded her arms. "Yeah, but if we can't get into the Clubhouse because magic doesn't work the way it's supposed to, we can't depend on transport bubbles, either."

"What about potions?"

All heads turned to look at Emily.

Nickie frowned. "That came outta left field."

"Not really," Laura said. "We have a few things to fill you in on."

"Yeah, please do."

Chuck groaned. "I don't know if I can sit through another explanation. It's like a song on repeat. A song I never knew existed but is now changing every single thing I thought I knew about life."

"Okay, babe..." Nickie eyed her sisters before leaning forward to make her boyfriend look at her. "It's okay if you need a break. You wanna go lie down in my room?"

He let out a short, high-pitched laugh. "That sounds like the best thing ever."

"Good. Okay. You want me to come with you, or..."

"Nope." Chuck sat upright and turned to face her. He grabbed her face with both hands and fixed those baby-blue eyes she loved onto her brown ones. "I'm so glad you're okay." Nickie smiled and covered his hands with her own. "And thank you for telling me."

"You're welcome," she whispered.

He kissed her long enough to get across how much he meant it without stepping over the PDA line in front of her sisters, then released her. "Good luck figuring out...whatever it is you guys have to figure out." Chuck stood and squared his shoulders. "I'm gonna go upstairs, and maybe after I've slept on it for a minute, I won't be the useless human who knows about magic but can't actually help."

"You're not useless, Chuck," Emily said.

"Yeah, right now I am. Don't worry, though. I'll change that. Somehow." He nodded at Nathan, who returned the silent gesture of acknowledgment, then headed across the living room toward the staircase in the foyer. "'Night, everybody."

"'Night, Chuck." Emily waved, though he didn't see her.

"Get some rest," Laura added.

Before Chuck reached the staircase landing, Speed slipped inside through the dog door and trotted through the living room after him. The bulldog snorted when he stopped at the guy's feet, and Chuck shot him a wary glance. "Yeah, okay. Come on, you immortal stink machine with fur."

No one said anything else while they listened to the creak of Chuck's slow steps up the staircase, across the hall, and toward the side of the house right above them, accompanied by the click of Speed's paws on the hardwood floors. When Nickie's bedroom door opened and clicked shut again, all three witches and Nathan let out a collective sigh.

"You guys really did tell him *everything*," Emily said, flicking her finger toward the staircase.

"At this point, Em, there's no reason not to." Nickie let out a heavy sigh and leaned back against the couch. "I just hope that when everything sinks in a little more, he doesn't just disappear."

"Do you mean literally…"

"No, Em. I mean run away and never talk to me again."

"Got it."

Nathan cleared his throat and shifted around to cross

his other ankle over the opposite knee this time. "I think he took it all pretty well."

Laura frowned. "The guy's in shock. We don't know how well he'll take it for a while."

"I've seen worse."

All three sisters turned to look at Laura's part-Kashgar friend. "Like what?" Emily asked, raising her eyebrows in intrigue.

Nathan chuckled. "Okay, so one of my cousins, he's the youngest of seven, actually, didn't really inherit magic like the rest of us."

"Huh."

"Yeah, I guess it happens. Maybe. I guess his whole family tried to keep theirs a secret for as long as possible, and the guy *lost* it when he walked in on two of his brothers building a school project with...you know." He lifted his hand and wiggled his fingers.

"Lost it how?" Nickie asked.

"He actually *did* run away. Didn't come home for a month, and I guess that was when he figured out how to wake up his own peabrain. Somehow." The sisters stared at him, and he shrugged. "I mean, so he didn't inherit the Kashgar magic. But the rest of him still knew what it was, deep down. Woke him up, I guess."

"I don't think that happens very often," Laura said.

"Right. But my point is that Chuck sat here through everything and didn't run away for a month. Or longer."

Nickie scratched the side of her head. "You think Chuck knowing about all this stuff is gonna wake him up to his own magic, too?"

Emily shrugged, and Laura came to sit beside her

younger sister. "You didn't tell him about humans and their magic, did you?"

"No. I know I can't do that."

"You guys didn't tell him what was gonna happen to his best friend when the Gorafrex moves on to another host?" Emily folded her arms and stepped toward them. "'Cause that might make him run."

"Yeah, that's what I'm worried about."

"Don't be, Nickie." Laura rubbed her back and shot a quick glance at Nathan. "That guy's head-over-heels in love with you, magic or no magic. If he understood why you didn't tell him about any of this until you had no other choice, he'll understand about Peabrain magic too."

Emily nodded. "Yeah, that's my guess."

"We'll see." Nickie pressed her lips together and gazed up at the ceiling. "Right now, he's up there wondering how he's gonna deal with everything we told him today, and I don't know if either one of us will be able to handle it when he finds out he's got magic too."

"But you can't do anything about it now," Nathan said. "You guys have a bunch of other stuff on your plates, and it's probably better to focus on that, right?"

Laura glanced at him and felt her face flush. *He's perfect.* Her cheeks grew hotter when she realized she'd had that thought.

"Yeah." Nickie bumped her shoulder against Laura's and peered at Emily. "So...you guys have some stuff to fill me in on since I heard the drums?"

Her sisters nodded. "My date with John went right down the crapper. I'm not really sure what—" Emily froze and blinked rapidly. "Wait, you said the drums hit you like an hour ago?"

"A little more than that now, but yeah."

"Oh…crap."

"Emily?"

The youngest Hadstrom sister clenched her eyes shut and blew out a long breath. "Laura, one of the energy cores we haven't gotten to yet doesn't happen to be anywhere near Emma Long Park, does it?"

"Hold on." Laura pointed at the middle of the living room, and her silver legacy ring flashed purple before the magical map she'd drawn out of the escape pod and all twelve energy cores appeared midair in the center of the room. She glanced at the northernmost dots on the circle around Austin and nodded. "Yeah, looks like there's one right underneath the park. Why?"

Emily smacked her forehead. "That's what that was."

Nickie stared at her younger sister, then glanced at Laura. "I feel like we're all on different pages."

"Yeah, not anymore. Something happened at the park, didn't it, Em? I mean besides Rutilda."

Nickie coughed in surprise "You met the Engineer at the park?"

"It wasn't on purpose." Emily tilted her head from side to side. "She kinda burst up out of the ground by the museum and stormed across town *toward* the park. Now I think I know why she picked that place." The youngest Hadstrom sister bit her lip and had a little bit of trouble getting the words out. "I'm pretty sure the Gorafrex got another power core up and running."

Laura huffed out a sigh. "Great."

"Okay, but we destroyed seven of them, so it can't launch the escape pod." Nickie nodded, trying to stay optimistic. "We still have that going for us."

"Except for magic's gonna start rockin' the boat like a crazy person."

Nathan pressed his lips together and forced himself not to laugh at another one of Emily's vivid analogies. "What does that mean?"

Laura slapped her hands on her thighs, stood, and nodded at him. "It means we need to hurry."

CHAPTER TWENTY-SEVEN

The next morning, Nickie picked up her full cup of fresh brewed coffee and leaned back against the counter. She blew over the rim of her cup, then took a sip, making sure to slurp it extra loud.

Laura grunted and shifted in her chair. She and Nathan had fallen asleep at the kitchen table sometime in the early AM with their heads cradled in their arms, and an old, handwritten book open on the table among a few scattered papers with a bunch of rune drawings over every inch of available space.

Nickie slurped another sip. Nathan puffed out a sigh but didn't stir much more than that. The middle Hadstrom sister reached behind her for one of the kitchen drawers, pulled it slowly open, then slammed it shut.

Laura's head jerked up and she gasped. Nathan sat upright and sucked a sharp breath through his teeth. They both looked completely out of it.

"Hey, good morning." Nickie smiled and held her coffee cup with both hands again. "Anybody want some coffee?"

"Uh…" Laura blinked and cleared her throat. She squinted at Nathan still there sitting across from her and frowned. "What time is it?"

"Little after nine. What time did you guys…well, I guess hit the table instead of hitting the hay, huh?"

Laura glared at her sister and shook her head. "Leave the bad jokes to Emily. It's way weirder when you do it."

Nickie chuckled and pulled two mugs down from the shelves.

Nathan cleared his throat and slapped his cheeks a few times. "I last remember being awake around four."

"Yeah, that sounds about right."

"You guys definitely need coffee, then." Nickie stepped aside and gestured to the empty cups. "Help yourselves." Her sister and the part-Kashgar rose and shuffled toward the counter like a couple of zombies. "Was it worth it?"

"Huh?" Laura squinted at the cup Nathan poured for her and picked it up with an eagerness bordering on desperation. She didn't bother with cream and sugar. After a few sips, she sighed and nodded. "Yeah, I think we picked apart which pieces of the rune are used for which purpose."

Nathan lifted his mug to his lips and chugged the hot coffee right there in front of the counter. Lily and Nickie shared a surprised glance, and when the man was finished, he let out a huge sigh and turned to fill his mug again. "At least we pinpointed which lines stood for the bond between living being and technology. We just have to pick apart a few others and figure out how to add the transference bit and the command to put the Gorafrex back *into* the prison before activating the original rune that kept it there in the first place." He looked at Nickie and lifted his mug toward her. "Good coffee, by the way. Thanks."

Nickie blinked for a few seconds and couldn't help but smile a little. "Yeah, I can tell you like it." They all headed to the table and took a seat.

Laura stacked a few of the loose papers and slid them to the side before setting down her coffee and cradling it in her hands. "I think we only need, what, another couple hours before we can find all the pieces we need. Then I'll stick the rune on the iron lance, activate it, and *voila*. Instant Gorafrex teleporter."

"Okay. A few hours is good." Nickie nodded. "'Cause we should hit as many energy cores as we can today. Emily said it's fine if we go without her."

"Where did she go?"

"Work. When her shift's over, though, she said she had an idea for a potion she thinks will work. I honestly don't know how that's gonna pan out."

"I mean, potion-making is almost like cooking, right?"

The witches stared at Nathan for a few seconds, digesting his statement. "Yeah, I guess. In the same way that physics is like parachuting out of a plane."

Laura snorted into her coffee and pointed at her sister. "Okay, that one was pretty good."

Nickie smirked. "If Emily makes whatever potion she thought up out of nowhere, we'll take that with us when we go out tonight. Hopefully, everything will work the way we need it to, considering how many things are starting to not work." She set her elbow on the table and crossed her fingers.

"Yeah. Let's just hope we don't run into any extra problems—" Laura stopped at the sound of footsteps pounding down the stairs.

Chuck rounded the corner into the dining room and headed for the kitchen, his hands shoved all the way into the pockets of his jeans. "'Morning." It was cheery enough, but his voice sounded rough, like he had a head cold.

Both witches and Nathan lifted a round of tentative, curious greetings; none of them knew how he was going to act the day after finding out he'd been lied to for a long time. The only sound in the kitchen came from Chuck opening and closing the cupboard door, setting his own mug on the counter, and pouring himself a cup of coffee. He opened the fridge in silence, grabbed the half-and-half, fixed his cup, and returned the carton all without looking at them.

Laura caught Nickie's gaze, and her sister shrugged a tiny bit, her eyes wide. But Chuck brought his coffee with him when he sat at the table between Laura and Nathan. He took the first sip, glanced at the papers on the table and the open journal, and nodded. "How's the rune coming?"

Blinking in surprise, Laura nodded in return. "Uh... pretty well, actually. We were just saying we probably only have a few more hours to find all the other components, but it shouldn't take long."

"Good." Chuck looked at Laura, then at Nickie. "What about Emily and her potion?"

Nickie sat back in her chair, realizing he'd done exactly what he said he'd do the night before. *He's definitely not useless. Just testing how far he can take all this.* "She had to work this morning, but she said she has a plan for that too. I really don't think it'll take her long. Emily's great at focusing super intensely for short periods of time."

"Yeah, that makes sense," Chuck said with a smidge of sarcasm, then took another sip and smiled. "Coffee's good. So, you guys are gonna find Dave tonight, right?"

"That's the plan, yeah." Laura nodded, then turned toward her sister and pointed at her. "Hey, we actually *know* Dave."

Nickie's eyes grew wide. "We sure do."

"No, I mean we can track *him* down. Not the Gorafrex, obviously, but we can get something of Dave's and follow it to wherever he is."

"Oh...huh. You think the singing bowl will work for that?"

Laura shrugged. "Worth a try. I mean, it worked when we were looking for the first witch that thing kidnapped, and she was already..." She stopped and shot Chuck an apologetic smile.

"She was already what?"

"She was dead when we found her."

Chuck slumped in his chair. "Oh, come on."

"Babe." Nickie leaned forward. "Dave's fine. He's not a wizard, and witches and wizards are the only beings the Gorafrex is after. The only ones it's trying to kill, I mean. As far as we know, all the other hosts were fine when that thing let them go. And it *will* let Dave go. I promise."

Her boyfriend glanced back and forth between the sisters and huffed a sigh. "You've actually seen the other...hosts?"

"Yep." Laura nodded. "There are only three we know of, but we were there when every single one of them woke up after the Gorafrex left. They were fine." *Minus the mind-blowing realization that they now have an awake peabrain that lets them access magic.* "There might be a little healing involved, but nothing serious."

Chuck swallowed, stared at his coffee, then sat forward. "Okay. Sounds good to me." He took another sip and scanned the work Laura and Nathan had stayed up poring over. "Anything I can do to help?"

"Nothing comes to mind right now," Laura said.

"But we'll let you know if something comes up. Thanks, babe."

"Yeah, well, I always try to help you guys as much as I can. You know that."

"And you've never let us down, Chuck." Laura flashed him a cheery, genuine smile.

"Right." He nodded and drummed his fingers on the table. "I'm gonna go home and take a shower. Text if you need me. Actually, maybe text me if *anything* happens? Otherwise, I'll worry."

"Sure."

"You got it."

After draining the rest of his coffee, he stood, bent to kiss Nickie goodbye, and pulled away just enough to say, "I love you."

"Love you too."

Without another word, Chuck walked back through the dining room toward the front door, which he closed silently behind him on his way out. Nickie sipped her coffee and stared at the table.

"Yeah." Nathan nodded and slid the old journal closer to get started on the rest of their work. "I'd say he's definitely taking it well."

CHAPTER TWENTY-EIGHT

E mily's phone went off again when she was halfway home after her opening shift in the kitchen of Meadowlark Tavern. When she stopped at a red light, she glanced at the screen to see a text from John: *'At least Ansler's not screaming at everyone again. People are starting to forget about Sunday's dinner party for swingers. Wish I had more than ten minutes with you in the parking lot.'*

She smirked and tossed her phone onto the passenger seat. "Yeah, me too. That's what happens when everyone works food and bev. Not a lotta room for a social life." The light turned green, and she floored the gas pedal. "I promise I'll have more time once we get this stupid Gorafrex taken care of."

The rest of her trip home took most people eight to ten minutes, but she made it in six. Her wheels screeched a little when she pulled up to the curb, but she rarely noticed that part of her driving, either. She slammed the door shut, jumped up the stairs two at a time, and burst inside the house, expecting to see everyone gathered in the living room or the kitchen.

"All right. I know you guys are done with all the heavy-lifting rune stuff...Hello?" No one answered, and after a quick search, she realized the house was empty. "Huh. Probably better anyway. No distractions."

She pulled up a group text to her sisters. *I'll be in the greenhouse. Shouldn't take long. Potion on the way.'* Feeling optimistic about the whole thing, she nodded, stuck her phone in her pocket, and headed into the foyer.

"Okay." Emily rubbed her hands together and squinted at the staircase. "Let's see what that overgrown garden can whip up." The walls rumbled and shifted around her, the staircase folded in on itself, and after a few seconds of sliding and falling and turning, the house pulled up the glass door into the magically hidden greenhouse. "Here we go."

The moment she stepped inside, Emily thought the house had mistaken her request. "This is a forest..."

Except it *was* the greenhouse. The glass panels making up the walls and ceiling were barely visible through the thick curtain of vines crawling over every surface. The tiled floor was more cracked and shattered than two days ago, and the plant that had grown teeth on its leaves and tried to eat Nickie's hand had actual fangs sprouting from its blooms. "Yeah, they do kinda look like mouths. Things are really getting outta hand."

Emily ducked under tree branches and stepped over jutting roots and ferns exploding from the floors. When she reached the far end of the greenhouse opposite the door, the worktable was fortunately still there. "If this is magic acting all weird, at least the furniture hasn't grown legs and walked away." She knocked a few times on the wooden worktable and nodded. "Just in case. Okay. I know Mom left some supplies. They gotta be around here..."

After a few minutes of opening and closing various drawers, she finally found the one she wanted. "Yes. Okay, this would be one of those moments where I'm actually glad Laura's so infuriatingly organized." She pulled the huge, worn potions book from one of the bottom drawers and brushed leaves off the table to clear a space. "First-time potion. Nice experiment. I can do this." The pages felt brittle between her fingers, but the recipe book wasn't nearly as old as the tome of Peabrain magic Laura had been lugging around for a year.

Emily ran her finger along the potions listed on each page. "Instant cleaner. No. Sound-canceling...nope. Hair growth? What is this, Potions for Homemakers?" She took a deep breath and settled her frustration. "I'll find it. If this thing was organized anything like an actual cookbook, I just need to find the right section. Totally doable."

The bush with the red and purple leaves and mouth-shaped blossoms shuddered behind her with a whisper of a rustle. The other plants in the greenhouse muffled most of the noise, even when a thin, dirty-yellow vine snaked its way from beneath the leaves and slid out onto the floor. Each mouth-shaped flower on the bush opened wider, exposing the fang-like thorns, and the vine crawled toward the unsuspecting witch.

· · ·

Emily stood at the worktable another ten minutes, sifting through various potion recipes. A few had seemed relevant to what she needed, but none felt right. "I'll know it when I find it. Just gotta keep...what? Who in their right mind would use a potion to *give* someone acne? Never mind. No time to figure that one out."

Behind her, the vine crept along the ruptured tile floor, slowed down by the other plants reaching out to strike at it as it snaked along after its prey.

"Oh! Yes!" Emily slapped her finger down onto the page and grinned. "Returning stolen things. That's it. Let's see... good for physical items, secrets, dreams...*stolen* dreams? Woah. Identities, voices, wishes. Yeah, okay. This is it. So that calls for...weird." She turned around as the tip of the yellow vine rose up like a snake to strike. Another mouth-shaped flower bloomed at the very end, opening wide petals like huge jaws.

The young witch jumped and moved her hand to bat the thing away before thinking better of it. Her legacy ring did the rest of the work. The copper ring flashed a bright-green light that slashed through the air. The vine let out a hiss and dropped to the floor before retracting all the way back to its bush on the potting table.

Emily stared at it. "You know magic's seriously messed up when your own plants turn on you. Maybe they wouldn't if we spent more time in here *tending* them..." Her gaze fell upon the gaping red flower on the floor, those fang-like thorns snapping against each other. Finally, the thing's reaction slowed until it was barely moving, severed from the end of the vine that had tried to take a bite out of her.

Emily hummed in approval and bent to scoop the thing up. She pinched the back of the flower to keep it from flipping over and sinking fangs into her fingers, but she carried it to the worktable and set it down far enough from the book it couldn't damage the aged pages.

"Now for the super professional supplies…" The next drawer she opened contained an endless selection of glass vials. "Just like my spice rack, huh?" She grabbed one that looked like it could hold thirty milliliters and thumped it down on the table. With a warning glance at her copper legacy ring, she found her place again in the recipe for Returning Stolen Things. "Don't let me down now. We're just getting started."

An hour later, Laura and Nickie looked up from where they sat in the living room as the house rumbled and churned, walls sliding into place, retracting, unfolding, and rearranging. When the wall blocking off the foyer slid sideways toward the front door and disappeared, Emily stood in the foyer, clutching a vial of a sparkling orange substance and grinning. "I totally rocked this, by the way."

"Emily!" Laura shot up from the couch and gaped at her youngest sister. "What the heck happened to you?"

"I mastered my first potion. That's what happened." Emily shrugged off her sister's concern and danced into the living room.

Nickie laughed and instantly bit it back. "How many times did you blow yourself up before you *mastered* it?"

Emily scoffed. "I don't know what you're talking about. I didn't blow anything up, break anything, destroy property, *or* lose important information. I made us *the potion.*" She stopped in front of the coffee table and thrust the potion at her sisters. "For returning stolen things."

Laura and Nickie stared at the vial of sparkling orange. "Em, it's not like we're trying to get back a wallet or a car..." The oldest Hadstrom sister tilted her head.

"What? Yeah, I know that. Come on. This also works for..." Something brushed across her arm, and she looked down to see a bundle of pine needles walking down her forearm toward the vial in her hand. "And, by the way, the greenhouse has seriously gotten out of control." She brushed the needles onto the floor and stomped them into the area rug. "I didn't even see any pine trees."

"Obviously, things got weird in there." Nickie stood and pulled handfuls of leaves—both green and brown—from her sister's tangled hair. "Really, though. You look like you blew something up and got tossed into a forest."

"That's exactly what it is in there. *But* I found Mom's old potions book." Emily grinned.

"That's *right...*" Laura sat back against the couch cushion and laughed. "I organized that whole worktable before we all got too busy to even bother with gardening."

"Yeah, well, we had more than enough for me to make this." Emily shook the vial at her sisters, then pumped her arms in a victory dance.

From the armchair on the other side of the coffee table, Nathan cleared his throat.

"What the—" Emily jumped away from the chair and did a double-take. "You're *still* here?"

Nathan laughed, and Laura gave her little sister the death stare.

"Yeah, I'm still here. Laura and I finished the rune. Then she and Nickie went off to successfully break another energy core, I think. Right?"

"Oh, yeah." Nickie nodded, a smile spreading over her face. "It was successful all right. Took a little longer than normal, though."

Emily pursed her lips. "Magic problems?"

"Probably."

"Hey, how's Chuck doin', by the way?"

Nickie blinked and took a deep breath. "Chuck's…adjusting."

"I think it's already sunk in for him," Nathan said. "He's been running errands all morning."

Emily squinted. "Errands for us?" Her sisters nodded. "Huh."

"And he brought Dave's toothbrush." Laura nodded at the coffee table.

"That's definitely a toothbrush. Wait, why does Chuck have Dave's toothbrush?"

Nickie snorted. "I'm pretty sure he pulled it from the guy's office, Em."

"Oh…uh, why do we need his toothbrush?"

Laura took a deep breath. "We're gonna use the singing bowl. Find Dave that way, and then use our weapons and the rune-imbued lance and your potion there to get that thing out of Chuck's friend and back behind bars, so to speak."

"Right."

"Is it an actual singing bowl?" Nathan leaned forward and grinned. "I love those things."

"This one was made by a Tibetan monk. I can't

remember how many hundreds of years ago." Laura shook that little memory frustration out of her head. "It tracks magical frequencies back to the source. In this case, an item's owner."

Emily crossed her arms, gently squeezing her potions vial. "We had an actual wand last time we used that thing. A toothbrush isn't exactly a magical item."

"It is when it's been in a Peabrain's mouth." Laura raised an eyebrow. "Even if that Peabrain doesn't know what he can actually do."

"Yeah, okay. Sounds like it's worth a shot. When are we headin' out?"

"We were just waiting for you. We should probably get going. Less time for magic to turn itself inside out, right?" Nickie slapped her thighs and stood from the couch. "I'm so ready for this to be over."

"You can say that again." Emily nodded at the part-Kashgar sitting in their living room. "You coming?"

Nathan's eyes widened before he shook his head. "Nope. My work here, at least until Laura asks for my help again, is done." He dusted off his hands just for show and leaned back in the armchair. "I'd totally like to see that singing bowl in action, though."

"Done and done." Laura stood, snatched up Dave's toothbrush, and nodded at her sisters. "The Clubhouse is stocked. We'll grab everything we need from there before we hit the one-mile mark, right?"

As if they could read each other's thoughts, the Hadstrom witches all turned at the same time and headed for the front door.

Nathan pushed to his feet and blinked. "Yeah. Sounds good." But they were already out the door, so he hurried after them.

CHAPTER TWENTY-NINE

In the passenger seat of Laura's car, Nickie held the magic-tracking singing bowl in her lap and swirled the red-tipped mallet around the bowl's rim. The sound of it reverberated through the car, even with the driver-side door open and Nathan peering over Laura in the driver's seat. "That sound, right?" He looked at each of the sisters with an enthusiastic grin. "I could listen to that all day."

In the backseat, Emily folded her arms. "You obviously haven't heard it nonstop in a car while tracking down a magical being."

"No..." He frowned at her. "Is it that bad?"

Emily tipped her head at him and didn't say a word.

The singing bowl glowed with a red light before it overflowed and shot the magical tracker through the windshield and northwest across Pressler Street. "There's our direction." Nickie set the mallet in her lap and nodded.

"Time to go." Laura looked at Nathan and smiled. "Thanks for all your help. We wouldn't be doing any of this right now without you."

"Naw. You would've figured it out. But I like that I wasn't just getting in the way." He leaned down until his face was inches from hers. Nickie turned over her shoulder and shared a wide-eyed glance with Emily in the backseat. "Get rid of that thing and come back in one piece. Got it?" Laura's smile widened into a full-blown grin. "You be careful, Professor Hadstrom."

"I always am." For a few seconds, all three witches thought the part-Kashgar physics professor was going to make his move and kiss Laura right there in the car. But, he just nodded and stepped back. "Let me know when we can celebrate you guys finally finishing this thing." With that, he shut the driver-side door and walked around the back of Laura's car toward his blue Jeep parked at the curb.

Laura gripped the steering wheel with both hands and blinked.

"Wow." Nickie eyed her older sister with an appraising smirk. "I'm impressed."

"Yeah, and I don't think he meant celebrate, like, all of us together, either." Emily scooted forward and peered around the driver's seat. "He was talking about just the two of you. Alone."

"To celebrate," Nickie added.

"Well…good." Laura grabbed her seatbelt and buckled it before shifting into drive. "I wouldn't have invited either of you anyway."

Her sisters laughed as Laura drove them up Pressler Street toward downtown, following the general direction of the red light that had shot from the magical-frequency tracker in Nickie's lap.

. . .

Half an hour later, Laura glanced at the singing bowl and nodded. "We have to be pretty close. Try it again."

Emily groaned and plugged her ears.

Nickie drew the mallet around and around the bowl's rim. With the metallic ringing came another flash of light. They'd gone through the flashes of red, orange, and yellow as they drove closer to wherever the Gorafrex was hiding out. Nickie almost didn't register that the light shooting out of the bowl and almost straight in front of them was white. "That way." She pointed, then blinked.

"Hey, that was white," Laura almost shouted. "You guys saw that, right?"

"Yep."

"Totally white."

"We're almost there." Laura pulled over on the side of Barton Point Drive in the Barton Creek West neighborhood, parked, and turned off the engine. "Got your charms?"

Nickie and Emily pulled out their keyrings and gave them a little jingle.

"Good. Let's—" Laura took a deep breath, then unbuckled her seatbelt. "I'm gonna do this outside."

"What? Why?"

The oldest Hadstrom sister pulled her keys from the ignition and opened the door. "That lance isn't gonna fit in my car without poking someone's eye out." She shut the door, and Nickie and Emily both chuckled.

"Yeah, okay." They each got out to stand on the sidewalk with Laura, and all three thumbs slipped over their individual thumbprints on the round silver charms.

"Wow." Emily gazed at the pile of their Gorafrexhunting paraphernalia in the center of the Clubhouse. "You guys weren't kidding about being prepared."

"No, we leave the jokes up to you, Em." Laura stepped toward their things and hefted the long iron lance, its full silver color flashing under the orbs of magical light on the ceiling. "Didn't get to show you this, though."

"Watch it." Emily leaned back when her sister brought the tip of the lance toward her, then she grabbed the end and lowered it from her face. "Hey, nice rune. Looks like a Christmas tree floating on a whale's back."

"What?"

"You know, Em, I was thinking more along the lines of a pineapple sorta cut into four pieces and rearranged." Nickie pointed at the rune etched into their big sister's iron weapon. "But I totally see where you mean about the tree."

Laura scoffed and lifted the sharp tip into the air again. "You guys are ridiculous."

Laughing, Nickie bent to grab her Strat off its stand and looped the strap over her head and shoulder. Her free hand clutched the handle of the small portable amplifier she'd used the last time they went up against the Gorafrex, and she turned to face her sisters. "Ready when you are."

Emily eyed her up and down. "If you had a giant trekking backpack on right now, you'd look more like a Ghostbuster Rockstar than a Hadstrom witch." She and Nickie had a good laugh over that, while Laura just shook her head.

"Doesn't even make sense."

"Okay, okay." Emily grabbed her single remaining iron orb and the leather half-glove and pulled it onto her hand.

Then she stuck the potion vial in her back pocket and tucked the orb under her arm. "Does it feel like we're missing something?"

"Oh." Laura went to the bookshelf and grabbed one of the jagged iron daggers her ring had made for them with no explanation whatsoever. She handed it to Emily. "Nickie doesn't have any free hands, but just in case we all have to pull a weapon…other than six strings and a pick."

Rolling her eyes, Emily took the dagger and pointed it at Nickie, shaking it up and down as she spoke. "This one's for you. But only if you need it."

"I won't need it." Nickie patted the body of her navy-blue electric guitar and nodded. "We totally got this."

"Okay, let's go."

The street was quiet when the sisters popped into exis-tence beside Laura's car. The sun was setting on their right, and most people living in the nice residential neighbor-hood were most likely sitting down to dinner or finishing their meals.

"Okay, let's not get sloppy." Laura flicked her hand toward Emily, and her silver legacy ring flashed. The same light shimmered over the iron orb tucked under Emily's arm, the dagger in her hand, and then the lance in Laura's. "Someone's gonna call the police if they see us walking around with this stuff. Come on."

The sisters headed down the sidewalk, knowing Dave and the Gorafrex were less than a mile away and straight ahead. After a few minutes, Nickie chuckled. "I don't think

I've ever had to carry my gear this far before. We usually just roll up to a gig and park in the back."

Laura glanced at the houses on either side. "We can't exactly drive right up to the thing and expect it to give us time to set up."

"Ha, ha."

The road curved to the left, and they found themselves at the end of a well-kept cul-de-sac that looked like a traffic circle. "Um...no Dave." Emily frowned.

"But there *are* more paths farther up there." Laura nodded at the narrow sidewalks branching off the street and disappearing through the thick trees. "We're at the edge of a Habitat Preserve."

"Should've brought the singing bowl with us." Nickie scanned the trees for any sign of spells or Gorafrex weirdness or electric-green sparks of an energy core. "How do we even know the thing's in there?"

A high-pitched wail rose from the trees ahead. The sisters glanced at each other.

"That's how we know," Laura said.

All three took off running down the closest path toward the sound of a wizard being sacrificed for an ancient machine.

They dashed through the trees toward the screams, which were coming from off the path. Nickie tried to keep branches from snagging on her guitar, and Laura did the same with her lance. Emily pressed the button on her iron orb, grabbed the thin metal chain that dropped from the open hatch, and cast the spell to bind the thing to the metal plate in the palm of her glove.

"Somebody help!" the man shouted. "Can anyone hear me?"

The sisters burst from the tree line into a round circle of cleared earth.

"Woah." Emily skidded to a halt and leaned backward just before her shoes tipped her forward over the edge of a massive crater. It went at least twenty feet down, and at the bottom was the witch who'd been screaming at the top of his lungs.

"What is going on?" Nickie muttered.

"That's an energy core." Laura nodded at the thing they instantly recognized; this one, though, lay on its side, half-buried beneath the earth, stretching across the entire diameter of the crater. The Gorafrex's next victim knelt beside it, his wrists bound behind his back in ropes of pulsing red bubbles. He tipped his head back to shout again and saw them.

"Hey. Hey! Please help me! He's gonna—"

A transport bubble appeared beside the terrified wizard. It popped, and Dave stepped out toward his victim. Only it wasn't exactly Dave.

Nickie set the amp at the edge of the crater, plugged the cord into her Strat, and nodded at her sisters. "This is it."

"Wait, how are we supposed to get down there?" Emily whispered.

"Em." Laura raised her eyebrows. "Levitating charm. On yourself. That thing's gonna know we're here in about two—"

They didn't even have two seconds. Dave's head tipped back, and his silver-flashing Gorafrex eyes caught sight of them.

"Now!" Laura leapt from the edge of the crater, her ring flashed, and the levitating charm slowed her descent enough to not break her legs when she landed.

Nickie turned on the amp and struck a chord. The sound launched Emily into action too. She jumped, though it was a lot less prepared than her sister's leap, and her copper ring blinked rapidly a few times without effect. She opened her mouth to scream as the ground rushed up to meet her, then her ring got a grip again and caught her just two feet from the bottom. Her feet thumped into the dirt, she stumbled forward, and then they were in front of the Gorafrex.

The thing snarled through Dave's lips. "Even witches have grown more stupid over the centuries."

Emily scowled. "Hey!"

The Gorafrex's hand shot toward her, but before it could unleash its attack of dark magic, Nickie burst into a frenzied version of the lullaby their dad sung to them every night when they were kids. The sound sent the Gorafrex reeling back, its eyes flashing silver. "You still don't have what you need," it spat. "But I do."

The creature's primal drumbeat splintered the air, battling the volume of Nickie's guitar. In two seconds, she'd matched the rhythm of the chords for the Hadstrom lullaby to the Gorafrex's witch-snaring magic—and its only defense. When Nickie played the song her ancestors had used to lock it away thousands of years ago, the Gorafrex's drumbeats lost their power.

The wizard kneeling beside the energy core stared at the odd display.

"This is the last time." The Gorafrex reached out for Emily as she wound her arm back to throw her iron orb. A storm of dark bubbles swirled from the outstretched palm and darted toward the youngest witch, but Laura raised her hand in time to deflect them. Her ring flashed a violet light that burst across the ground and drove the Gorafrex's attack away from her sister and back toward the caster.

Blood magic pelted Dave's body like rubber bullets. He stumbled back before tripping on an upturned tree root. Dave sprawled out across the dirt, and Emily glanced at her sister.

"Laura, he's gonna feel all this later."

"Yeah, I know, Em. There's only so much I can do to protect him."

Under its own magical attack, the Gorafrex took a few seconds to collect itself within Dave's body, but this weakened and the ropes of dark magic pulsing around the captured wizard's wrists burst and disappeared, leaving behind a rancid odor like bad cheese. The wizard scrambled to his feet.

"Here." Emily had enough time to toss the iron dagger at his feet before the Gorafrex pushed itself back up and hissed at them.

"You've failed every time," it snarled. "This is no different." At the same time the wizard grabbed the dagger, the Gorafrex rushed Laura. Emily launched her iron orb at the creature and propelled it with her legacy ring. Any other throw wouldn't have curved the orb the way it curved around Dave, wrapping around and around, up and down and diagonally, until the orb reached the end of the chain and thumped against Dave's pinned-down arm.

The Gorafrex stumbled sideways, and Emily tugged on the chain in her hand to tighten the slack. "We've been practicing."

Those silver eyes flashed as it twisted Dave's head over his shoulder. "For how long, *witch*? I have had thousands more years."

"That doesn't change a thing." Laura nodded at her sister while Nickie's fingers flew over the strings of her guitar above them, sweat dripping down the sides of her face. "Keep it up, Nickie!"

Emily tugged the potion vial out of her back pocket, popped the cork, and threw it at Dave. Sparkling orange liquid splattered all over the man's hair and the back of his neck, dripping over his clothes and onto the dirt at his feet.

Nothing happened.

A low, menacing chuckle rose from the man's mouth, and it didn't sound like Dave's laughter. It grew until the Gorafrex threw its host's head back and cackled. "All this trouble. For a—" It choked, blinked wide eyes, and growled.

The shimmering, opalescent aura they'd seen every time the Gorafrex was about to switch bodies pulsed in a giant flash around Dave. It sucked back into the man's skin, and a piercing shriek rose from his mouth.

The wizard had stepped up beside the creature and tried his hand at stabbing his abductor in the side. "No, no, no!" Emily shouted, but no damage struck Dave's body. Not while the Gorafrex was inside. The dagger thumped to the dirt, bloodless and clean, and the wizard backed away.

The shimmering aura flared, and Laura made her move. She brought the tip of her lance up against Dave's chest, pushing hard enough to feel the pressure but not break skin. Hopefully.

The creature's drumming increased in a last attempt, but the sisters' magic had done its part. The swarm of Gorafrex consciousness lifted from Dave's body, wriggling and struggling, and bent toward the rune in Laura's lance. Dave screamed.

The trees around them in the preserve groaned and shook, despite even a hint of wind. The ground trembled, and Nickie stumbled over her amp. Her boot nudged it just enough to send the thing hurtling down into the crater, and the cable yanked out of her guitar. She cursed but kept playing.

When the ground cracked at the bottom of the crater, Laura and Emily had just enough time to leap back before a huge, jagged shard of rock burst upward, separating them from the Gorafrex. Laura's lance lost contact with Dave's body. The chain wrapped around him jerked Emily forward.

"Bring him back!" Laura shouted and reached out toward Dave before the Gorafrex escaped. Her ring flashed. Instead of grabbing Dave with her summoning spell, she ended up pulling a huge chunk of rock out of the ground. It flew toward her, and she jumped out of the way before it crashed into the wall of the crater.

Emily's copper ring sputtered and crackled, undoing the binding spell she'd used to seal the end of her iron chain to her glove. The chain whipped out of her hand, and Dave fell backward.

Nickie's black legacy ring strobed a series of blinding purple lights, and two of her guitar strings snapped and almost whipped her in the face.

The trees glowed, and the sisters thought they heard all those thousands of voices rising from the very real, very living thing rooted into the ground. It sounded like rage.

Without their planned magic to keep it where they wanted it, the Gorafrex flung itself from its host, launched into the sky, and darted over the trees until it vanished from sight.

Dave groaned at the bottom of the crater, still tied up in iron chain. The front of his shirt bloomed with tiny pinpricks of blood where the Gorafrex's dark spell had backfired. A much more alarming stain spread by a second wound on his side. The wizard had done enough damage with the dagger; it was just now showing up.

"Nickie, get down here fast," Laura shouted.

Nickie lifted her guitar strap over her head, set down the Strat, and jumped over the edge to join them. Her ring alone didn't do nearly enough to help slow her descent, but her sisters joined in. So did the wizard, who'd had enough presence of mind to pull out his wand and use it this time instead of an iron weapon he knew nothing about.

When she landed at the bottom, Nickie stumbled forward and kept running until she slid to her knees beside Dave. "Okay, okay. *Please* work this time." With magic acting completely nuts, none of them could be sure her healing spells would work, despite how much they'd improved as she learned to use her legacy ring. Nickie took a deep breath, pursed her lips, and blew over Dave's body.

It took a few seconds for the purple healing bubbles to burst from her mouth, but they finally did. One by one, they floated over Dave's body and settled atop the countless wounds that had destroyed his shirt and peppered his flesh, and the bleeding ceased. The air filled with the scent of lavender.

Dave's eyes fluttered open. When he saw all three Hadstrom sisters and a complete stranger standing over him—not to mention the fact that the entire world flashed in brilliant colors now that his tiny magical brain had been hijacked awake—all he could do was mutter, "Woah."

Then, his head dropped back onto the dirt, and he passed out again.

The sisters stared at each other for what felt like a long

time. "Okay." Laura clicked her tongue and frowned at Dave. "Looks like we're back at square one, huh?"

"We were so close." Emily hung her head and closed her eyes.

"We'll figure it out, Em. Who wants to start working on a transport bubble first?"

It took them ten minutes to finally get their magic to do what it was meant to do before their twenty-sixth attempt grew a bubble large enough for three witches, one wizard, and a newly awakened Peabrain.

CHAPTER THIRTY-ONE

"Em, how can you even be sure about this?" Laura nodded at the fairy watching her and her sisters walk through the main library in downtown Austin.

Emily barely turned around to answer her. "Just a feeling, okay? Besides, it's not like it has anything *specifically* to do with the Gorafrex."

"Hey, maybe keep it down about...the *thing*." Nickie glanced around and tried not to psych herself out about anyone watching them do anything.

"You guys need to trust me." Emily turned at the nondescript wall and walked through it. The magical barrier made her skin prickle a little, but she kept moving into the high-security magical books section. Her sisters followed behind her, and now that they'd stepped beyond into this magicals-only room, Laura and Nickie relaxed a little.

"What are we looking for again?"

Emily glanced at Laura and lifted her finger. "More potions, to start. Anything that has to do with making things *work* again, right? 'Cause magic isn't working for itself right now."

"Or us," Nickie muttered.

"Right. We know my potion worked. So did Laura's rune. If the world wasn't being scrambled by two and a half activated energy cores, we would've had the Gorafrex locked up yesterday."

"So what? We're trying to find something about potions that fix magic?"

"Yeah. Or that don't need much magic to do the same things magic *would* do if it wasn't already screwing up so badly." Emily squinted at a shelf and pulled down a thick purple volume. "Because potions, as far as I know, are the only tools that don't rely completely on magic. The rest is alchemy."

"Actually, Em, that makes a lot of sense."

The youngest Hadstrom sister turned toward Laura and winked. "Rutilda helped me with that one. So let's keep—"

The library shuddered. A massive explosion rocked the center of downtown Austin. The Hadstrom sisters rushed toward the window at the far end of the magical books section and peered outside. A massive plume of purple energy billowed into the sky. Car alarms went off. People stopped to stare, ran the other way, screamed, or moved as fast as they could while glancing over their shoulders.

Emily flinched when a lamppost fell out of the sky and landed in front of the window, clattering onto the pavement of the library parking lot. She turned toward her sisters, who echoed the same expression of surprise and disappointment.

With a sigh, Emily shrugged and tried to smile. "We have a *lot* of reading to do."

The End

Magic in Austin is officially on the fritz, and there's no way to predict what a spell will actually do. Now, the Hadstrom sisters have to turn to older methods of fighting the Gorafrex, but none of them have any real experience with making potions. Can the trio of witches fulfill their family legacy and set things right? The adventures continue in <u>Magic Trinity!</u>

Get sneak peeks, exclusive giveaways, behind the scenes content, and more.
PLUS you'll be notified of special **one day only fan pricing** on new releases.

Sign up today to get free stories.

CLICK HERE

or visit: https://marthacarr.com/read-free-stories/

It's almost Halloween when I'm writing this and I'm headed to two parties tonight, which for me is unprecedented! I'm even dressing up as a 1920's flapper and I haven't gotten into a costume for a party since my early 20's – a very long time ago. (No, I haven't gotten into a costume since then for any other reason, either. Fortunately, Craig Martelle hasn't come up with that idea yet for a 20Books convention.)

First party is at the legendary amenity center about a quarter mile from my house. It's legendary because I've written about it ever since it opened last July. It's nicer than our houses and the HOA is continually throwing parties there with bands, food trucks and a cash bar. I've made the joke that we are all back in college, just with nicer dorms this time. Tonight's party is called Boos and Booze and there's a costume prize that maybe I even have a chance at winning.

Then my neighbors Alex and Vanessa are throwing

their annual party that others tell me is legendary. No costume, no entry. I'm hitting it early before the serious drinking starts and heading home by ten. A big night for me, which you'd think the Offspring would know by now.

Last night we had a pretty typical Texas rainstorm for this time of year. Sudden and intense and creating flash flooding. The whole area is soil on top of bedrock so there's no place for water to go. My area was hardest hit and just down the road is the flood zone. Frankly, that was a selling point for me because no one can build there leaving a lot of green space.

The Offspring, who rarely answers his phone called to ask if I was okay, but it was past ten at night. I was fine and asleep. He became alarmed and had Jackie Venson, his soon to be wife and famous blues guitarist, call me even though she was sitting next to him. He must think I screen my calls, but I always answer his. Wait, we're not done. Then he called the neighbors and asked them to drive down the street and ring the doorbells. By the way, they weren't under water so why would I be and why didn't they point that out? And did I mention my doorbell doesn't really make a very loud sound? Then they called another neighbor to see if they knew where I was.

By the time I woke up and saw my phone a lot of my neighborhood was looking for me. It's nice to know that so many people care, including the Offspring. It also answers my question about whether I could die and dissolve into the floorboards before anyone would notice. I'm happy to report they'd find a warm corpse most likely. Happy Halloween everyone! I'll be sitting outside with the bowl of candy next week with the good dog Lois Lane and sweet Leela barking their fool heads off in the window behind me. May all of you have a festive evening as well. More adventures to follow.

OTHER BOOKS BY MARTHA CARR

Other series in the Terranavis Universe:

The Adventures of Maggie Parker
The Adventures of Finnegan Dragonbender

If you enjoyed this series, you may enjoy these series
in the Oriceran Universe:

THE LEIRA CHRONICLES
I FEAR NO EVIL
REWRITING JUSTICE
SCHOOL OF NECESSARY MAGIC
SCHOOL OF NECESSARY MAGIC: RAINE CAMPBELL
ALISON BROWNSTONE
THE DANIEL CODEX SERIES
FEDERAL AGENTS OF MAGIC
SCIONS OF MAGIC
THE UNBELIEVABLE MR. BROWNSTONE
THE KACY CHRONICLES

OTHER BOOKS BY MARTHA CARR

MIDWEST MAGIC CHRONICLES
SOUL STONE MAGE
THE FAIRHAVEN CHRONICLES

OTHER BOOKS BY JUDITH BERENS

OTHER BOOKS BY MARTHA CARR

OTHER BOOKS BY MICHAEL ANDERLE

JOIN THE TERRANAVIS UNIVERSE FAN GROUP ON FACEBOOK!